Suitable Precautions

Suitable PRECAUTIONS

Laura Boudreau

BIBLIOASIS

Library and Archives Canada Cataloguing in Publication

Boudreau, Laura, 1983–
     Suitable precautions / Laura Boudreau.

Short stories.
ISBN 978-1-926845-29-6

     I. Title.

PS8603.092675S85   2011   C813'.6   C2011-903436-0

 Canada Council   Conseil des Arts    ONTARIO ARTS COUNCIL
for the Arts   du Canada   CONSEIL DES ARTS DE L'ONTARIO

 Canadian   Patrimoine
Heritage   canadien

Biblioasis acknowledges the ongoing financial support of the Government
of Canada through The Canada Council for the Arts, Canadian Heritage,
the Canada Book Fund; and the Government of Ontario through the
Ontario Arts Council.

PRINTED AND BOUND IN CANADA   BIO GAZ

This book is for Larry Garber, as promised.

CONTENTS

The PARTY

TRY THE MUSHROOMS, he says. They're barbecued in their own juices. There are people eating
the mushrooms, holding their cocktail napkins
like offerings. Yes, their own juices, one of the women says,
touching her fingertips to her chest in a way that makes me
reconsider grilled vegetables. The walkway is crowded and
people turn to slide past one another, chest to chest, as they
edge over to the girl with wine-stained lips who asks, Red
or white? and then looks at you disapprovingly if you reach
into the ice-filled garbage can and fish around for a beer.
Or maybe she only looks that way if you dry your hand on
her tablecloth when you think she isn't looking. But we are
all friends here, and so what is a little impropriety among
friends? The plastic sheeting canopy protects us, even though
there is nothing but sunlight falling from the sky, and in
the cozy haze of not-yet-dusk we meet each other again
and again and for the first time and say, by way of intro-
duction, How is it that you know Mary? And have you tried
the mushrooms?

You look beautiful, someone says to someone else. And it must be true because there can be no lies on a patio where people are whole-face laughing about a punch line that goes, But I thought you were writing a novel! I look around to make certain, and sure enough we are beautiful. Even the man in the rumpled brown suit who is spilling his glass of wine is beautiful. He pinballs around the party, bumping into chairs and bouncing off elbows, veering towards a woman with a short skirt and particularly freckled legs. I am a poet, he tells her, emphasizing the "am." Yes, I believe you, the woman says. She says it with the sort of kindness that only ever comes from concerned strangers and friends who have seen you naked. The poet sloshes a few drops of wine onto her legs. The spots blend with her freckles.

And because there are no lies here, I almost believe it when a man says to me, Don't I know you from somewhere? I know I've seen you before. And he seems so sure that without even really meaning to I say, Yes, I believe you. My one small lie, if it is one, goes unnoticed on the patio, what with the sun having nearly set and our shadows looking alike and blending together. Maybe that is the source of the confusion, if there is any. This new familiarity breeds conversation between me and the man who knows me from somewhere. Quickly we make intimate exchanges of shadow space and pheromones and business cards. When we are done, he asks me, Have you had anything to eat yet? Because all I see are mushrooms. I can't think of anything to say except, I have to go to the bathroom. I say it with the indeterminate sort of kindness that comes from trying not to trip on uneven patio stones while intoxicated.

A sad-eyed woman sings on the stairs in the living room, accompanied on guitar by a man who sticks his tongue out in concentration as he strums. They are in love it seems, even though she looks right at him when she sings, Did you ever go clear? When the song is done and we have clapped until the sad-eyed woman has kissed her guitar-strumming man, a poet who is not in a rumpled brown suit reads a poem that has a line in it about being so happy that sunshine shoots straight out of your asshole. You know it! shouts one woman, who is, luckily, sitting down. There is one more performer, and his story ends with the words, You can start running the bath—I'm coming home, which is a beautiful way for a love story to end, Mary says. The band fires up. The bagpipes are loud, but Mary has taken suitable precautions. And you would never know that Alec from next door only started playing tambourine tonight.

A man with a camera is photographing a woman's foot. The woman, happily flustered, has removed her shoes and pointed her toes with unexpected humility, five-alarm-red polish excepted. In some cultures, the man says as the shutter clicks, the feet are considered the most beautiful part of the body. Ankles, the woman says as she reties the laces of her espadrilles, are power. A man is dancing barefoot in the kitchen, probably because it seems the only decent thing to do under the circumstances, and I can see his ankles. They are hairy. The photographer does not seem interested. We collide in the kitchen, me and this dancing man, and he says to me, Promise that you will never watch where you are going. We laugh in time to the music. Excuse me, someone says as I am dipped by the dancing man, but you're blocking the sink.

A man in a Honk If You're Going To Hit Me t-shirt and cycling shoes is asleep on the couch. Mary is calling him a cab. I could use a whisky, a woman with a baby in her arms says, and Alec, putting down the tambourine, knows a place. There are plans. We say to each other, It was a pleasure meeting you, as we try to find our jackets and handbags. We kiss each other on the cheek or on the mouth, depending on the precise level of our pleasure. One last wine glass is accidentally smashed in celebration. We realize that punctuation is everything. People stream through the front door, mouthing cigarette smoke into goodbyes and thank yous, and through the haze of all our exhalations we make our way to the street.

Strange PILGRIMS

THE FIRST TIME ELLA MET CHARLIE he gave her the letter. She had just moved into the little blue house with flaking white trim and a leaky basement. She had looked all over the city at three-floor Victorians and coach houses in alleyways, bungalows built just after the war and sterile new condos, and the little blue house, though not her favourite, was what she was able to afford. It had a backyard with a garden and thick grape vines that separated her from the embankment where teenagers met to smoke cigarettes and drink beer they stole from their parents. The house had three bedrooms upstairs. The front one was small but sunny, just the right size for a crib and a rocking chair, perfect if Ella ever had a baby, her mother said. The kitchen came with a new stove and a fridge that had recently had its compressor fixed, and outside there was a wooden shed where Ella could lock up her bike for the winter and store potatoes when it got above zero. It was a good house, Ella thought, and so what did it matter if she heard the train through the single panes of glass at night?

"Thank God for train tracks," Ella's father had said as he took the bank manager's pen. Ella was lucky. There was no question about that.

Ella was stacking boxes when the doorbell surprised her. She had tried the dented button the week before and it hadn't worked, so she had posted a sign for the movers that was still there, the Scotch tape cracking from the cold: Knock loudly. Yet there was the bell, chiming a metallic intrusion. Ella was struck by the newness of the old house and annoyed by everything she still didn't understand about it. Her real estate agent, a fat man who wore perfectly tailored suits, had said something about property taxes, something Ella had forgotten to write in her notebook, and her mail was still not being redirected from her old apartment. The only thing in her mailbox was a notice of an outstanding hydro bill in the name of Matilda Giacoma, but when Ella called the company hotline to explain that she was the new owner, Charlene the chatty service representative had asked for information Ella didn't have: what was her new account number and security password, did she like the new neighbourhood, and could Ella please spell her mother's maiden name? Ella had hung up the phone, ashamed she didn't know how to spell Wojnarowicz.

"I'm coming," Ella shouted as the bell rang again and again, interrupting itself.

"Shovel," the mailman on the front step said as Ella opened the door. He handed her a stack of letters, their yellow and black address labels stark against the whiteness of his unmittened hand. He almost looked young enough to have a mother who might still scold him for this. "I don't get paid to break my neck out here."

Ella flipped through the mail. Junk offers and a puffy envelope from her grandmother. A belated birthday card, probably, with a five-dollar bill camouflaged in a stack of tissues. "I've been waiting a week for these." Ella tried to sound indignant. "I paid thirty-six dollars for the redirection service."

"Sometimes they collect a bit before we send them on," the mailman shrugged, his jacket swishing. "Shovel your walk, lady. Then maybe you'll get your mail faster."

Ella stood on the steps as he cut across her lawn to the next house, his boots punching holes in the pristine whiteness of her yard.

"I just moved in," Ella called to his back, but he raised his arm and shook a pack of letters without turning around and Ella shut the door feeling lost. She didn't even own a shovel.

She put her grandmother's letter on the mantle and tossed the rest into a pile by the fireplace. A pale, creamy white envelope, lovely in a stark way, stuck out against the flyers. She had missed it before, perhaps because it was so small, hardly bigger than a deck of cards. She ran her fingers over the heavy paper, tracing the postmark. *Roma.* It was addressed to M. Giacoma.

Imagine, Ella thought, sending a letter all the way across the ocean only to have it arrive too late. She didn't know what to put on the envelope. "Return to sender" seemed vague and "Recipient deceased" too brutal. She thought about it for a moment before taking a pen out of her purse: "No longer at this address."

The mailman was a jerk, Ella decided as she put the pen behind her ear and went back to work. She was tired of men like that. Men with bad tempers and superiority complexes. Still, she made a plan to salt the walkway later in the afternoon and buy a shovel. But only if she found one on sale.

Ella balanced a box of old books on the stairs. One day she wanted to line the living room with heavy oak bookcases, organizing them according to her own secret system, but for now she only had one cheap bookshelf that had been damaged in the move—dropped out of the truck, the base of it cracked—and she didn't have the money to replace it right now. The books needed to go somewhere. It was depressing to see them in beaten-up liquor boxes in front of her fireplace. She was going to pay off her debts, have bookshelves and side tables and things on the walls. Paintings. She might take up painting. In the meantime, the front bedroom was empty and it might be a nice place to read, if she found a chair to put in there. I should check out the attic, Ella thought as she reached the landing. Maybe there was a chair in the attic. Even if there wasn't and it was just more empty space, it was still hers. She owned it.

The attic was supposed to be insulated and dry, good for storing Christmas lights and all kinds of other things she didn't own. Ella wasn't expecting the blackness of the old wallboards to be broken by a bright hole the size of an intrepid raccoon or an especially industrious squirrel. A small cascade of snow lined the hole while insulation spilled out of crevices and twisted around strips of newspaper that curled themselves into a balled up nest of the past. There was an ad from Sears: a picture of a woman in a blazer with wide shoulder pads and high-waisted pants; modern fashions for women, twenty percent off.

Ella had paid for a house inspection and her house had passed with flying colours, but what did they look for if not giant holes in the attic? She had no idea where she was going to get the money for repairs, not to mention the exterminator.

There was more than just mulched newspaper and insulation in the nest: there were oddly beautiful bits of paper, purple, blue, green, red, ripped up and kaleidoscoping through the design. Ella had heard stories of animals moulding all kinds of things into their nests—parking tickets, strips of bloody gauze, scraps of love letters—but it wasn't the strange colours that made her plunge her bare hands into the mixture, ignoring thoughts of rabies and lice as she picked out shreds of paper and pieced together the feral jigsaw puzzle. It wasn't the frustration of discovering yet another problem with the house beside the railway tracks she didn't have the money to deal with. It was the pale green face of a young Queen Elizabeth from a worn twenty-dollar bill.

There were six hundred and seventy-four pieced-together dollars when Ella had finished picking the nest apart. She kneeled on the floorboards and looked at the waste of the chewed bills, the sting of it like a nail gnawed to the quick. The tears were in her eyes before she realized that the six hundred and seventy-four dollars weren't important: the insulation and the newspapers were from the attic. Her attic. Empty and hers. Ella wiped her eyes with the sleeve of her sweater and looked out into the blank white void of the hole in the wall, then down at the warped floorboards. Several of them were loose and she started ripping them up by hand.

SHE DIDN'T KNOW EXACTLY how much money there was. The animals had done a number on the waterproof bags, tearing open their plastic bellies and letting the bills fall between the joists like discarded paper bones. Each bag held about ten thousand dollars and she had found fifty-four bags so far. She was trying to be sensible about it—a twenty for bread and eggs, butter and milk, a fifty for dinner and a night out at the movies, maybe—but the whole thing didn't make sense. Ella woke up in the middle of the night and moved portions of the money around, hiding six bags in the flowerpots in the locked wooden shed, then hauling four of them into the kitchen, suspending them down the old laundry chute and painting over the door with the spare can of paint she found in the basement. She opened a safety deposit box to store six more bags, and the bank woman who smelled of hairspray asked her if she would like a private room to deposit her valuables. "Yes," Ella had said, sweating through her blouse, "some privacy would be nice," as though she were talking about a hospital room for risky elective surgery.

A dozen bags between the springs of her old couch, and eight more in the cubbyhole under the stairs. Ella had spent the better part of a night in the garden, hacking at the frozen ground with her new shovel, boiling pots of water to soften the earth, and now there were ten bags buried in the best garbage bags she could buy, housed in waterproof camera cases, ten more under the grape vines in plastic containers Ella bought from Canadian Tire after having been assured by both the teenage salesman and the department manager they were completely waterproof. She made a map of the backyard and mailed it to her grandmother, asking her not to open the sealed envelope. She left two bags in the attic, mostly because she wasn't sure where else to put them. Ella knew she was being strange about it, but she couldn't help thinking and rethinking her hiding places. She bought seven fire extinguishers, one for every room in the house.

She quit her secretary job at the insurance brokerage. "I have a family emergency," she told her boss. She spent her time trying to find out the story of the money, dogged by guilt and fear, wondering if Matilda Giacoma had hidden a fortune from her greedy children, or been involved in some Italian crime syndicate. Ella spent weeks scouring old newspapers and looking through public records at city hall only to find out that Matilda Giacoma had lived in the house for nearly forty years and had no family to speak of. A sister in Europe, one of the checkers-playing women at the community centre thought, but no, definitely no children. Matilda had died after a long battle with cancer, according to her obituary, and Ella's neighbours were going to miss her at the street party this year—she made such tasty lemon tarts.

Not sure what else to do, Ella started going to church again. She lit a candle for the eternal soul of Matilda Giacoma and said prayers of apology. Several times she considered going to confession. It wasn't a sin to be lucky, she told herself. She wasn't a graveyard ghoul—the money came to her. Ella spent a lot of time counting, wondering if she was blessed or cursed.

After a few months, Ella started to feel comfortable with the money. She bought herself a new pair of boots without feeling like she was going to throw up, and from there she felt strong enough to buy a silver necklace and a matching bracelet, then a mahogany bookshelf from an antique market and two reading chairs, one for the sunny front bedroom and the other for the living room, to go with the new bookcase. She repaired the hole in the roof and hired a pest removal service to deal with the animals in the attic. Raccoons, it turned out. The lanky man arrived wearing thick, industrial gloves, carrying a trap that looked hardly large enough for a well-fed house cat. She paid cash upfront and then tipped the man forty dollars when he came back with a whimpering raccoon, its fur poking wildly out of the cage bars. "Can you take good care of him?" Ella asked.

"Don't worry, lady. They always get taken care of," he said, putting the cash in his shirt pocket and bashing the cage against the door frame, his shoes leaving a filthy dance pattern on Ella's linoleum hallway as he stepped around yesterday's mail. It was a pile of mostly junk flyers, even though she had repeatedly told the mailman not to deliver them. "Your junk, your problem, lady," he said, and no amount of nasty looks from Ella or complaints to his supervisor had made a difference.

"Sorry about that," Ella said as she picked up the stack, her hands recognizing the heavyweight paper a moment before she read the name, the words stopping the air in her lungs: M. Giacoma. Postmarked in Rome.

Ella quietly shut the door behind the exterminator and locked it. She closed the blinds in the living room and sat in her new reading chair, her blood thudding in her cheeks and her fingers cold and raspy against the smoothness of the cream envelope. It didn't mean anything. There was nothing to mean. It was just a letter, a mistake. Someone who didn't know that Matilda had died. It was sad, that's what it was. Sad and that was all. Why was she worried? What was there to worry about? This was her house and she had lived in it for months. She hadn't done anything wrong. No one had blinked twice at the antique store when she paid cash for the bookshelf. She had been downright honest, telling the salesman he had undercharged her by sixty dollars when he rang up the bill. And who was to say the letter had anything to do with the money? Imagine an old woman with a body full of cancer hauling bags of money up those rickety attic stairs and prying up the floorboards with hammers and crowbars. It was ridiculous. She was being ridiculous.

Ella took a deep breath and looked at the envelope. The penmanship was strong and dynamic: thin, hard, written with urgency, Ella could tell. The return address on the back was carefully scripted. No smudges. Each letter clear and precise, but spiky, impatient for an answer. Whatever was inside was important. Beautiful, maybe. Sad, almost definitely. Nothing at all to do with Ella or the money. A coincidence of address, just like the hydro bills that still came to her house addressed to M. Giacoma.

Ella took her pen out of her purse. "Recipient deceased," she wrote on the envelope. She just hadn't been clear enough the first time.

Ella slipped the letter in the mailbox that afternoon, along with a large donation to the Toronto Humane Society. She returned her new boots and gave the money to Girl Guides selling cookies on the street corner, their cheeks pink and their teeth new and white.

If the letter came again, she was going to ignore it, Ella decided. Throw it away and that was it. It had nothing to do with her or her new life.

Ella had told her parents she had landed a job as a ghost-writer for nearly famous people who wanted to write their autobiographies but couldn't. A lack of time, maybe, or talent, she said. Ella's father tried to get her to talk about her work when they went out on Sunday afternoons.

"Oh, look at this one," he said, pointing to a glossy hard-cover as he and Ella browsed through the Spring Sale section of his favourite bookstore. "I wonder if it's any good."

"Dad, you know I can't talk about my work. It's part of my contract," Ella said.

"Oh, I know, I know. I just wonder." He walked over to another table and held up a book. "What about this one?"

Ella shrugged. "It's too soon for any of mine to be out, Dad."

Her dad bought the book anyway and made her sign it: To Dad, Who knows all my secrets.

Her mother shouted out names at random.

"Tom Cruise," she said.

"No, Mom. I don't get paid a Tom Cruise salary."

"Okay, Anne Murray."

"More like Anne Murray, but still no."

"Leonard Cohen."

"Mom, why would Leonard Cohen need me to write his book?"

"I'm just saying, Ellie, that I wish you got the credit for what you do. Those people you write for are just nobodies pretending to be somebodies. I bet they couldn't string two words together without you, but it's their ugly mugs on all those covers."

"I don't mind," Ella said.

It would have been true. Ella didn't mind anonymity. While people thought she was writing anonymously, she was living anonymously, cycling through the city on her rusted ten-speed, buying flowers and weaving them into the baskets of other bikes chained outside the flower shop. She bought fruit at the Chinese market. Ripe mangoes, raspberries that stained her lips, her thumb, her forefinger. In the first flush of spring she watched children in yellow rain slickers feeding ducks at the pond with day-old bakery bread. In the autumn she sketched the trees in the park, drawing them thin and bare with the curves of old women. But life was not meant to be this easy and beautiful, she was sure, and so every day she did something that disgusted her. She touched the severed pigs' heads at the meat market. She picked a cigarette butt off the ground and smoked it. That is worth some money, when you think about it, she said to herself. That is worth some money.

She decided she didn't want to know the story of the money. Good luck should make her thankful, not afraid. She had always been a lucky person, and fortune, so she heard, favoured the brave. In the thick heat of summer she had sewn a few hundreds into the lining of her good wool coat and felt courageous.

The letter arrived six times that year, the same little envelopes, the same handwriting, but Ella was firm—they went in the garbage, unopened, and she got on with her day. Buying lemonade from the neighbourhood children, tipping them each a dollar as the sour juice made her squint. Raking the leaves for Mrs. Robertson, who had arthritis and poor eyesight. Never leaving anything less than a twenty in the collection plate. Ella made a point of shovelling the fine, dusty powder on the day of the first snowfall. She wanted to bake her mailman cookies to apologize for things from the winter before. She thought about buying him mittens as a Christmas present, maybe red and navy ones to match his Canada Post jacket. His hands had been so pale, and this year she was making an effort.

"FIFTY-ONE CENTS IS NOT A LOT TO ASK," Charlie said. "Find me anybody else who would take a stinking letter from here to Saskatoon for fifty-one cents, and I'll be damned. You think you can go up to someone on the street and get them to take a letter down the block for that?" Ella said no, she didn't think so. "You're damn right," Charlie said. "You can't."

Dangerous dogs shouldn't be left to terrorize the neighbourhood.

He didn't steal pension cheques, so stop calling the cops.

People who didn't shovel their snow should try doing his job and not breaking their legs. Ella of all people should know that.

If he had had a bad day, he might go on for hours.

Ella went to the kitchen to get Charlie a beer, thinking for the hundredth time that no matter what, those gloves had been worth the money. Even now it seemed like an extravagant idea, cashmere lining and Italian leather, but she had talked herself into it and made a plan, knowing that it was a good year for grand gestures.

She had waited until a bad snowfall and then watched the mailman come up the walkway. When his boot hit the wobbly first step of her porch, Ella had crouched a little and jammed the small flat box through the mail slot. It was a tighter fit than she thought, and the shiny gold wrapping scraped most of the way off. She hung onto the corners of the box with pinched fingers.

"What now?" The mailman's voice came through the door.

Ella shoved the gift forward a little and lost her grip. The box slipped onto the porch and the brass flap that covered the slot snapped shut on the wrapping. Ella yanked the paper back and balled it up in her hands.

"Sorry," she said through the door.

She poked the flap up again with one finger and saw the mailman from the waist down. He turned the box over.

"They're mittens," she said, panicked. "Gloves, I mean."

He tucked the box lid under his arm and tried one, stretching his fingers inside the soft leather.

"Fits like a glove," he said, reaching his hand closer to the mail slot. Ella didn't laugh.

The mailman kicked at the salt on the steps, which were scraped down to the bare concrete. Ella wasn't sure what to do next.

"I'm hungry," he said. "What about you," he checked the letters in his bag, "Ella?"

They spoke through the mail slot. Ella said they should meet at the pasta place on the corner when his route was done.

"No, I'll pick you up," he said, sliding the mail to her, waiting for her to take it before he let go. Ella had felt stupid as the flap clanged shut and the mailman walked away. Her calves were cramping and she had forgotten to ask for his name.

But it didn't matter now, Ella thought happily, popping the cap off the beer. Charlie loved her just the way she was. She was his. "Charlie, Charlie, Charlie," she whispered to herself as she padded back to the living room and handed him the bottle.

"A cold beer and a hot woman," Charlie said. "This is heaven, right, babe?"

Ella said that it was. She stretched her legs out along the couch and let him balance the bottle between her bare ankles. When it spilled, he licked it off her skin, careful with his tongue as his hands pushed up the leg of her jeans. He spilled more on her shin, licking as he went. The blond hairs on Ella's thighs stood up from the cold and so she took the bottle and began pouring. Down his chest, over his waist.

They licked, drunk on expectation, and Ella rushed to take off her panties before they were doused in beer, knowing the way the cheap fabric stained. She wrapped her legs around him tightly; it so often seemed that Charlie was just barely tethered to her, that when they made love he was in danger of gliding over her and disappearing.

She washed his uniform in the sink, the washing machine broken again and the beer stains setting. First his shirt, then his pants, which she hung over the shower curtain rod to dry. She cleaned everything. Washed her hair, the beer bottle. Once, after seeing a police show, she made Charlie scrub down the entire couch: if a crime were committed in the house and the police checked for bodily fluids, she knew she would feel unbearable shame, even if she were lying dead in the next room, her throat slit by a drug addict trying to steal her stereo.

"You're crazy," Charlie said to her, "but I love you."

Ella kept washing her hair.

She bundled him up for work on winter mornings, taking care to tighten his scarf, reminding him to bring his gloves. He never left the house without an extra pair of socks in his bag, in case of rain. "Happy feet make happy people," Ella said. In the summer Ella froze bottles of water halfway, alternating drops of juice from fresh lemons and limes into each distinct layer of ice. This was her definition of love.

It had stopped amazing Ella that she loved Charlie, really loved him, and yet lied to him the way she did. She read him poems when he couldn't sleep, and he brought her bouquets of dandelions from abandoned hydro fields. Sometimes they fought over the dirty dishes in the sink, and sometimes Ella was lonely and cried quietly, hoping Charlie wouldn't wake up and ask her what was wrong. They were in love in a very strange and troubled world, Ella knew, and the fact that they were happy was enough for her to know that the lie was worth it, that the work she did to keep it up was love itself. If one of the letters showed up in Charlie's mailbag, Ella said nothing about it and threw it in the garbage. She stopped bugging Charlie to go to church on Sundays. She had found faith.

Ella knew there was a paradoxical relationship between truth and lie: the more outrageous the lie, the more people believed it to be true; the more outrageous the truth, the more people believed it to be a lie. Either way, you believed. If you were lucky, Ella thought, the difference between the two eventually disappeared, and you kept standing in your bra in front of the bathroom sink, washing beer out of a uniform.

"I'm a ghostwriter," she had said over spaghetti on their first date. "Freelance."

It had been easy to lie, easier still to keep it up when Charlie moved in during Ella's second spring in the house. Charlie's salary was enough, and when it wasn't Ella made up the difference, pretending to ghostwrite. Ella imagined life as a rich woman, and she knew what it was like being a poor one, and now she was comfortable. That was the best so far. She and Charlie ate fish and chips on Fridays and thought about the names of their children, the ones they would have when they had saved a little money and maybe planted a tree in the backyard.

"How about Emily for a girl and Aaron for a boy?" Ella asked.

"When we have the money, babe," Charlie said. "But I like Emily."

Everything had a price. Ella discovered this to be true after Charlie told her he couldn't imagine his life without her, that he wanted to marry her. Ella started having dreams.

They were different dreams, but somehow always the same. In the first one, the house was burning down. The blue paint was glowing an electrified orange, melting in radioactive globs onto the lawn. The white trim cracked. The old wood split apart in violent explosions. Charlie was there, inside the house, and Ella was screaming, Charlie, Charlie, get out! But Charlie just stood there behind the broken screen door, shaking his head at Ella, his skin melting, mixing with the blue paint. In another, Ella and Charlie were on a sailboat. Ella with her hair around her shoulders, basking in the sun and watching Charlie turn the ship's wheel. A storm followed them. It pushed them closer and closer to the horizon. The force of the wind whipped Ella's hair across her face, drawing blood. Look, Ella, look, isn't it beautiful? Charlie asked her. He smiled in a way that made his skin taut over his skull. Ella could see all the way down to the bone.

"Baby, another bad dream?" Charlie asked when Ella woke up sweating in bed.

"Yeah," she said.

"What about?"

"Can't remember," she lied.

"It's just a dream, baby," he said. "Go back to sleep. I've got to get up soon."

The dreams became worse if she had used the money. On the day she spent two fifty-dollar bills on a new blue dress, she dreamed of hurtling towards the earth in a ripped-apart airplane. She kept trying to reach for Charlie's hand, but couldn't find it. The plane slammed into the water, and Ella felt herself drowning. She woke up coughing.

Unconscious guilt, she told herself. These dreams don't mean anything. But she knew otherwise. She let the droplets of sweat evaporate off her body and listened until Charlie's breath came slow and even out of his mouth, smelling just slightly of garlic. She got up and walked naked out into the garden to eat a handful of earth.

She started saving the envelopes that arrived from Rome, tying them with a red ribbon and climbing the ladder to the attic. She sat cross-legged on the dusty floorboards for hours at a time, thinking. Something needed to be done.

She wore her blue dress to their anniversary dinner. Charlie gave her a pair of beautiful green earrings, the colour of Ella's eyes, he said, and a card. On the front was a watercolour picture of two people holding hands and walking along a beach at sunset. Love is the air, the ocean, the land, it said. When she opened the card, there was part of an e. e. cummings poem that she liked written in Charlie's spidery handwriting:

love is the voice under all silences,
the hope which has no opposite in fear;
the strength so strong mere force is feebleness:
the truth more first than sun, more last than star.

Happy Anniversary, it said after that.

He signed it, For Ella, my sun, my star, my ocean. Love, Charlie.

She gave him the stack of letters in a cloth-covered box.

"What's this?" Charlie said, undoing the ribbon and flipping through the letters.

"You don't recognize them?" Ella asked. "You deliver them every once in a while."

"I don't know, babe," Charlie said. "If I looked at everybody's mail all the time, I'd go nuts. I don't even read my own mail. Most of the time I don't care what I put in the box as long as there isn't a cat clawing at my leg or some little old lady telling me I forgot her Sears catalogue."

There was disappointment in Ella's fingers as she rearranged her silverware on the clean white tablecloth.

"No, babe. Don't be like that. I'm sorry." He put his hand on hers. "Tell me what you're thinking."

"Well, you're supposed to give paper for the first anniversary," Ella said. "That's if you're married, I guess, but I thought it was a nice idea. I figured, what with you being the greatest mailman in the world and all, that we should return these. Paper, right?"

Charlie was silent.

"I thought it could be a love letter, or something," Ella said a little desperately. "Sent again and again from across the ocean. Imagine sending that and never getting a reply, never knowing what happened to your letter."

She wanted to tell him that returning such a letter would be an act of mercy. An act of penance. That she was planning to donate her dress to the Salvation Army. She wanted to tell him everything.

"But babe," Charlie said as he twirled an envelope in his fingers, "it's from Italy."

Ella reached into her purse and pulled out two plane tickets. *Roma*, they said.

"Ella! You're crazy. I knew from the beginning you were crazy. You were the one on the route that was craziest." He thumped the tickets on the table. "Do you know how many washing machines these could buy?"

Ella shrugged. "It's only paper, Charlie," she said. "Happy anniversary."

They got drunk and laughed all night long, but the next day Ella went to church and prayed to Saint Anthony of Padua, the patron saint of travellers and harvests, of seekers of lost and stolen articles. The patron saint of mail. The protector against shipwrecks.

I SHOULD TELL YOU, Ella almost said when Charlie took the letters out of his backpack again, but the noise of the train stopped her. She and Charlie had talked little since the rusty squeals of the engine had combined with the drunken songs of the cigarette-smoking men, three or sometimes four of whom hung out of the stuck-open windows, yelling obscene Italian to the *nonnas* with thick ankles who dotted the dried-out paths alongside the tracks. Ella had even stopped holding Charlie's hand, the clattering of their wrist bones against their shared plastic armrest not worth the effort. In the corner of the car, there was a chicken in a cage. A dog smelling of junkyard roamed the aisle. A nun lost herself in prayer as the ticket collector tapped people on the shoulder who pretended not to hear him.

"Strange pilgrims," Charlie shouted into Ella's ear.

"What?" she said.

"I'm glad we're here."

"What?"

He handed her a granola bar.

In Ella's guidebook to Italy there was a section on train travel. She had highlighted the prices, the connecting stations, the numbers to call for schedules and reservations, even though she couldn't understand the recorded messages she got when she dialled. Under her pens the map of inter-secting train lines turned into iridescent veins and arteries, criss-crossing the leg of Italy, their ink-blood pooling, it seemed, somewhere near Rome. All roads lead to Rome, the caption below the map said. The facing page had a health warning about deep vein thrombosis. There was no mention of chickens.

Charlie kissed Ella on the lips as the train pulled into the station. The men got off the train, leaving behind the virile stink of their armpits, dog fur, a few feathers. The nun stayed where she was. "This is it," Charlie said.

Charlie inched his way past the nun who was faking sleep. Ella looked at him and imagined herself having his children, taking care of him when they were both old and he was sick and thin from cancer and her eyes were milky white with cataracts.

"Ella," he said. "Are you coming?"

Ella put the highlighted guidebook into her bag, sure the nun was watching through the reptilian sliver of her right eye. Charlie helped Ella down the stairs and held her hand as they walked into the pearl pink sunlight that settled over the city. She held on tighter as they walked alone, together, into a stream of women on scooters, their hair unfurled; of men in pointy-toed shoes and dark sunglasses, saying, *Pronto, pronto*, into their cellular phones; of angels etched in the stone façades of banks and insurance companies.

Ella bought a carved giraffe from a North African man selling his goods off a tattered blanket. His hands, covered in pink and grey scars that snaked up his arms, touched hers when he gave her the figurine. "You will have good luck," he told her. She believed him on the grounds that a man with such scars would not joke about luck. Charlie hailed a taxi. The world now negotiable, it would never be flat again, no matter how many times Ella had dreamed of sailing to the edge of the earth and looking over.

The dreams had changed since she bought the plane tickets. The night before the flight, Ella had seen herself in fields of poppies, her feet bare and covered in earth. She heard Charlie's voice calling to her from a great distance. Look, Ella, look, he said. Isn't it beautiful? Ella's hair was long and tangled and touched the backs of her elbows, tickling her. But it wasn't her hair, after all. It was an avalanche of butterflies. Yellow. Black. They blocked her view of whatever it was Charlie wanted her to see. They flew in her eyes, into her ears. She could barely make out Charlie's words above the fervent fluttering of wings. In another dream she saw Charlie and a small girl playing in a park, the girl in a yellow rain slicker, feeding ducks. Charlie turned to look at Ella. With a shrug, he took the little girl's hand and walked away.

"Another bad dream, baby?" Charlie had said when Ella woke up breathing hard.

"Sort of. No. I don't know."

"Well go back to sleep, we're leaving early for the airport."

"Did you pack the letters?" Ella asked.

"Yeah, babe," Charlie had said. "Everything's fine."

Now, as Ella clutched the wooden giraffe in her hand and Rome washed over her through the window of the taxi, she knew Charlie was right. She was surer than ever that the world could be simple, could be beautiful. She and Charlie were going to return the letter. She was going to tell him everything. She was still working up the courage. She thought of them running up the crooked front walk when they got home, flinging open the door, laughing and kissing as she told Charlie the story again, tearing the rest of the lining off the old couch frame to show him the multicoloured paper that had given her nightmares. He might throw some of the bills in the air just to see them fall to earth, saying, Look, Ella, look. It's beautiful. They were going to plant a maple in the backyard and make love underneath it. Emily for a girl. Aaron for a boy.

"Okay, okay," the taxi driver said as he pulled up to their cheap hotel. "Okay."

"Wait," Ella said, turning to Charlie. "I think we should return the letters now."

"Now? Why don't we get settled, have some lunch, or something. I'm tired, babe." Charlie reached for the door handle.

"No," Ella said, grabbing his arm. "No, Charlie, please. We can't. We have to do it now. We have to." It was spring—why was it so hot? The windows. Had the taxi driver closed the windows?

"Jesus, Ella. What's wrong with you?" Charlie took out his wallet to pay the fare. "We're here. Let's check in, drop off our bags, at least."

But Ella reached into his backpack and clawed for the stack of letters. She peeled one off and shoved it in front of the cab driver. "Here," she said, jabbing at the return address. "Here, we want to go here, right now."

The cab driver looked at her, then at Charlie who shook his head. The cabbie lit a cigarette. "Right now," Ella said again, clapping her hands, and the driver finally turned the key in the ignition. Ella, ashamed but pleased that the car was moving again, sat back against the seat and felt the sweat press into her thin sweater.

"It's lucky we decided to take a vacation," Charlie said. "You're about ready to crack."

The cab drove for only a few minutes through the weaving traffic of the city before stopping in front of a small cobblestone laneway off a street of gelato stores and panini bars. There was a derelict church on the corner. Ella saw that the old apartment doors lining the alleyway were made of thick, weathered wood, the door handles the heads of rusted lions, the door knockers the faces of angels. "Here?" she asked. The cabbie flicked his cigarette out the window in response.

"Will you wait?" Charlie asked the driver. "Keep the meter running on us. We're only going to be a minute. One minute. Okay, Ella? Can we be quick about this?"

"But Charlie."

"Ella, come on. Meter's running." He grabbed his backpack off the seat, fishing for the stack of now crumpled letters, one of them already in Ella's sweaty hand.

The cab driver unfolded a newspaper and lit another cigarette as Charlie walked quickly down the laneway, Ella trotting to catch up. Charlie checked the address and then stopped in front of a large wooden door, painted green, on the left-hand side. There was no doorbell, no knocker, and so Charlie, before Ella could stop him, pounded loudly with the heel of his hand.

"Charlie!"

"What?"

It was too late. An elderly woman opened the door, shuffling back a few steps in her sturdy black shoes, laced tightly, before jamming a small doorstop in with her foot. Ella looked at her old nylons, pilled and with a small run at the ankle, which disappeared under the billowing waves of her faded black housedress. Her hair, mostly grey, was still streaked black in places and tied back in a bun. She smelled vaguely of lilacs. She reminded Ella of her own grandmother. Maybe everything was going to be fine.

"Sì?"

"Hello," Ella said, forcing her lips off her teeth in a nervous attempt at friendliness. "Hello, do you speak English?"

The woman looked from Ella to Charlie and back to Ella. She shook her head and clasped her hands together.

"We're from Canada," Charlie said, "Toronto."

"Yes, Toronto," Ella said again quickly. "We live in Toronto and these letters," she took the stack from Charlie and held them out to the woman, "these letters come to us there."

The woman took the packet, undoing the ribbon. She looked at Ella again, then Charlie, then back at the letters. She shook them in her hand, asking a question.

"I'm sorry, but we don't speak Italian," Charlie said. "No parlo Italiano," he tried.

The woman asked the question again, then again, louder each time, until she was shouting at Charlie, then Ella, throwing the letters onto the street where they landed with a smack, scattering like a bunch of small white pigeons. The woman shuffled forward, one finely manicured finger, the knuckle swollen, pointing at Ella, so close that Ella was terrified she might actually touch her, that the force of that one finger might stop the wild beating of her heart, killing her instantly.

"I'm sorry, I'm sorry," Ella said as Charlie put an arm in front of her.

"Hey, lady. Back off, okay? We're just returning your mail. I'm a mailman."

The woman turned to Charlie, stomping her foot and then pointing to the letters, to herself, her apartment. She tugged at the material of her dress and pointed again to the letter, to the washing on the line overhead.

"I'm so sorry," Ella said.

"C'mon, babe. Let's go." Charlie wrapped an arm around Ella's shoulder. They walked back to the cab, Ella half turned around, tripping over Charlie's heels as the woman stood in the middle of the street, her words a flood of incomprehensible curses streaming along the cobblestones.

"Whatever, lady," Charlie called without turning around, shaking one hand dismissively.

"Charlie, don't. Please don't." Ella started crying.

"Ella, it's okay. It's not worth it. I see lots of weirdos on my route. That lady's nothing." He opened Ella's car door and slid in beside her. "Back to the hotel, please."

"Charlie."

"Seriously, El, don't let her get to you. Who knows what her problem is. Don't let it spoil our vacation, okay? It was a really good idea, the letter thing." He kept his arm around her until she stopped shaking, but Ella still wished they had never come to this street, never come to Rome. Charlie was wrong, she knew that now. It was a bad idea, all of it. How could she have been so stupid, so selfish? She should have left the money in the attic, moved out of the house, even. She couldn't tell him the story now, she thought. It was just too risky. This was crazy. She was crazy. She was. Why did Charlie love her? She didn't deserve it. It was all her fault and she was never going to be able to make it up to him.

Their hotel room was small with a low and crooked ceiling. The exposed wood beams made Charlie think of a church. They made Ella claustrophobic.

"I'll go get some fruit," he said adjusting the straps of his backpack as Ella sat gingerly on the bed.

"What? No, don't go."

"Oh, come on. You just need a rest. You're too sensitive about stuff like this. Relax and try to forget about that crazy woman. When I come back we'll have a shower and go for a nice dinner or something, okay?"

"Please don't go," Ella said. "I'm sorry."

"Babe," Charlie sat down beside her, "you don't have anything to be sorry about. I'll be back before you know it. You're just overtired. Take a nap. Look up something fun in your guidebook for tomorrow."

"Charlie, please."

"Just relax." Charlie said, the keys jingling in his hand as he kissed her on the forehead. "Dream of me."

She didn't. She lay on the bed and dreamed of nothing but blackness and silence, and when she woke up she wasn't sure that she had been dreaming at all. Maybe she had just been staring into the blackness of the windowless room, listening to the sounds of the waiters in the street restaurants serve dinner, clear the plates, close the doors and stack the patio chairs; the women walking away in their stilettos; the sirens of the police cars, the ambulance. They had all died away and now it was quiet, and Ella, sleeping or not, stared into the blackness and silence, waiting for Charlie to come back. She thought he might bound into the room with a bag of oranges and a story of misadventure, hilarious and unbelievable. Something about him getting locked in the walk-in freezer of a fancy restaurant, or maybe of him volunteering for a street performer's act and then finding himself stuck in the very box into which he was supposed to disappear. Would you believe it? he'd ask. Not a word, Ella would say back, the orange juice on her tongue tart, the flesh of the fruit between her teeth.

Ella turned on a light and checked the time. It had been hours since the woman had shouted at them. Cursed them.

Ella reached into her bag for the guidebook. She started looking up the telephone numbers of the local hospitals and police stations, whispering a short prayer before she dialled. She called, asking for anyone who spoke English.

HE MIGHT LIVE, if he's lucky, the doctor said. But the knife had pierced a lung, his stomach; it had cut through his liver and intestines, the most significant problem by far. There was a serious infection now and he had lost a lot of blood before he had been found. Ella should be prepared.

"For what?" Ella asked stupidly.

"He lost a lot of blood," the doctor said again. "And now he has a fever."

"Oh," Ella said. "Oh."

Charlie was sleeping. He was in pain, they told her. This was better.

Charlie woke up crying at one point. He grabbed Ella's hand.

"Babe, I'm so sorry, they took it all, they took it all. It happened and, and it, I—"

"I know, Charlie, I already know." Ella said. There had been the strange heat of the afternoon, Charlie walking down an empty street. Then three men, maybe four, if the old man in the flower shop was right, catching Charlie in a surprise embrace. Long-lost friends, maybe, meeting by chance on a street corner a long way from home. Charlie, holding his hands to his side as the boundaries between blood and air dissolved between his fingers, the splashes of red on the street an inevitable map to the doorway he was found in—a boy coming home from school, the first day with his own key, new, the bright metal tied around his neck with an old leather shoelace. The police had told her. They were very thorough.

She had told them about the backpack. How there was money inside it. Plane tickets. Passports. She said nothing about the letters. The police had apologized to her for the mugging, the younger of the two officers, the one with the better English, taking her hand as though it were a baby bird while he explained that Rome was a safe city most of the time. "It has its share of pickpockets," he said, "but a mugging like this is very unusual." He told her they were doing their best to find whoever did this. Could Ella remember anything else, anything that might be useful in the investigation? She sobbed into his shoulder as he held her, one hand softly patting her back.

The nurse prepared a needle as Charlie began to wake up.

"We can't go home, babe." Charlie cried like a boy, delirious with the recklessness of pain.

"We don't have to go," Ella said, stroking his hair as he fell asleep again. "We don't have to go back. We won't go. Okay, Charlie? I love you. I'll stay right here with you."

Ella stayed even though the nurses told her to go back to the hotel.

"I'm not tired," she insisted, afraid of what she might see if she closed her eyes. She ran her hand up and down Charlie's arm as he slept the thick sleep of those who might never wake up.

His fever spiked in the morning. The nurses put a tube down Charlie's throat and taped it to his lips. The doctor who had told Ella to be prepared asked for her signature on some papers.

"We're trying," he said.

Ella signed her name. "Can I keep the pen?" she asked. She waited until the doctor left before she kissed Charlie's ear. Then she went to the nurses' station for a piece of paper and an envelope.

Dear Charlie, she started.

She told him how much she loved the way he curled up behind her in the night, the swell of his belly rising and falling into the small of her back. She told him that she really did like his cooking. She didn't know why she said she didn't. She told him that her favourite colour was blue, and that's why she hadn't repainted the house. Your breath, she wrote, smells like garlic when you sleep, and I don't mind. She told him she was sorry. She told him about the money. The dreams.

I love you, she signed it.

Ella wrote the address of the little blue house on the front of the envelope in slow and thick handwriting. She took the guidebook out of her bag and looked up the nearest post office.

She understood now why it was that you had to write down what you were going to abandon, what was leaving you. Why you might have to write it over and over again and send it all the way across the ocean. Ella turned the letter over in her hands and tried to imagine the feeling of dropping it into a mailbox. She should be prepared. She would let it go quickly, she decided. The envelope with no return address would barely touch her fingertips, leaving her hand like some pale and lovely ghost.

The
DEAD DAD GAME

I LIKED THE WAY Nate told the story. He was happy to reel it off, starting with the part where Genevieve, his first mother, collapsed on the kitchen floor with a blood clot in her lung. "It only took a second or two for her to die," he said, slowly lowering his hand in a side-to-side motion as though his mother had been a piece of wind-blown paper. "She probably didn't even feel it." Nate was a baby when it happened, and he had almost cried himself to death by the time the landlord unlocked the apartment door. His father—our father—lived with my mother by then. The day Genevieve died, my mother was busy giving birth. "But don't feel bad, Elaine," Nate said to me. "You almost died, too. You were early."

It seemed obvious to us that Genevieve's death was a lot better than our father's. It was definitely faster and there were no hospitals or operations, and Genevieve didn't have to lose her hair or spend a lot of time throwing up into stainless steel bowls. My mother agreed with us on principle, she said, catching our eyes in the rear-view mirror, but either way it wasn't appropriate to make a sport out of it. "Death isn't a contest, you know. Everyone gets the same prize." She lifted one hand from the steering wheel to make the point as we drove through the cemetery gates. Genevieve and our father were in different sections, but my mother said it was still very convenient for visiting, even if the traffic in this part of the city was hell.

We remembered our father a little, Nate more than me because he was older. Our mother encouraged us to ask all the questions we wanted, which helped us make up a few more memories. No topic was off-limits when it came to our dead parents. My mother didn't want us to grow up feeling guilty or resentful about things we didn't understand. "Fear is the source of all disease," she said as she made our kale breakfast shakes. She wasn't sure what our father had been afraid of, and we knew the theory didn't apply as well to Genevieve, but Nate and I bought into it anyway. We had a lot of questions.

"Did he walk with a cane?" Nate asked.

"Yes," our mother said, scraping the clogged blades of the Cuisinart with a wooden spoon. "He tried, anyway. He didn't want a ramp out front. We'd already spent a lot of money on the landscaping."

"What colour were his glasses?"

"He didn't wear glasses, Nate. You know that."

"And what about his eyelashes?" I asked. I felt left out because I mostly remembered a shadow that smelled like Vicks VapoRub. "Did they fall out in clumps?" Nate said that our father had pink eye a lot and sometimes wore sunglasses to watch television.

"This blender."

The more questions we asked, the more my mother's face went strange. The bones in her jaw looked like they had softened and stretched. It was uncomfortable to watch her when she talked like that. I felt like we were scaring her, which was the worst thing you could do to a person, in my book. Nate was going on about radiation therapy and its scientific connections to superpowers, and my mother's face kept shifting, like I was looking at her underwater. She rested the spoon on the stovetop and rolled up the sleeve of her dressy black sweater to pick at the blades, and Nate kept firing question after question: Was our dad ever a Cub Scout? Did he drink kale shakes? Which one of the three of us did he love most?

Nate had once told me that mothers, as much as you might love them, were all the same. He said that if anything happened to my mother, another lady would adopt the two of us, maybe one of our aunts in Philadelphia or Newark. Women loved babies most, he said, but we were still little enough to be okay. "It's fathers who are the tough ones. Much harder to come by."

Nate was living proof. I heard the way my mother tucked him into the bunk above me, telling him to close his eyes, sleepy bird, and dream of flying over all the green places on the Earth, but he still had to play the Father-Son Scout Baseball Tournament with Mr. Crisander. Mr. Crisander did up all the buttons on his polo shirts and parted his hair down the middle. At Halloween he gave out toothbrushes. He said Nate could call him Captain as a kind of nickname, but Nate stuck to Mr. Crisander. Mr. Crisander lived alone next door with his pot-bellied pig Mickey, who had been starved by her previous owners to make her small. It had worked, to a point. Now she was about the size of our Aunt Jennifer's fat beagle, and she came if Mr. Crisander called her, but Mickey was a lot heavier than a dog and had stumpy legs. She couldn't catch a Frisbee to save her life. She also had a bad skin disease. Her raw, scaly hide showed through her black and white bristles. Sometimes she scratched against the stone pillar near the bottom of our driveway and her back oozed. Still, none of our friends could say they knew a pet pig, and she seemed to like us. Nate and I felt like we had to pet Mickey if we saw her.

"I found Mick through the SPCA," Mr. Crisander said as Mickey plowed her snout into our limp fingers. "People buy them and think they'll stay piglets forever." Mickey seemed like a good enough pig, but it made us uneasy that she rubbed against our legs, shimmying and squealing. She also had a bad habit of rooting in my mother's garden. "Leave that thing for long enough," my mother had said, throwing out what was left of her tulips, "and it'll dig up the dead." It didn't help Mickey's case that our mother told us to wash our hands after we touched her. It made us think certain things about Mickey, and about Mr. Crisander. Nate had recently mentioned he didn't want to go to Scouts anymore, and my mother said she had been thinking the same thing. "I mean, a father-son baseball game? What are we, Republicans?" Nate went to Science Club now, and he was collecting cans to save money for his own microscope.

My mother didn't mind that Nate kept a picture of Genevieve taped to the ceiling above his pillow. Genevieve had a big pink flower behind one ear and her nose was sunburned. He didn't really miss her, he said, because how could you miss someone you didn't have space for? I felt like I knew what he meant. This was why we didn't have questions about

Genevieve, why her death sounded like a grocery list of events and why we never played the game with her. It was our father who was the hole in our lives.

"Did he die in the morning or at night?"

"Morning."

"How did you know he was dead?"

"He stopped breathing."

"Did his heart stop beating, too?"

"After a minute, yes."

"What happened then?"

My mother's face was sliding out from under her skin. She whacked at the blades with the spoon.

"Fucking blender," she said.

She flung the spoon across the counter and it smashed into Nate's shake. We jumped as the glass hit the tiles and the spoon clattered under the dining room table. Gobs of kale splattered onto Nate's suit pants as the glass broke apart with a barely audible click. The three of us looked at the mess on the floor. I started to cry.

My mother quickly picked up the biggest pieces of glass, the clink of them in her hand like a stunted wind chime. "He was dead, Nate. Nothing happened then." She wrapped the shards in a sheet of newspaper and threw the package in the garbage. "Don't cry about the glass, Elaine. If we were Buddhists, we'd already think of it as broken. Now go put your shoes on and wait for me in the car. And don't pet Mickey if she's in the driveway."

The drive was quiet, just the sound of Stevie Wonder from the tape deck. When we got close, our mother sang along softly. Nate and I didn't look at each other. Instead we watched the people on the sidewalk and tried to guess their names. Nate said the woman with the puppy in her bike basket was a Shirley, but I thought she was a Tory. We agreed that the man with the bundle buggy full of wine bottles was a George. We couldn't quite decide on the woman with the fabric shopping bags and bunches of sunflowers. A Rebecca, we thought, or maybe a Donna.

"A Genevieve," my mother said. "You can always tell a Genevieve. Nate, do you feel like telling Elaine the story?" We knew this was her way of asking us to forgive her, which we did right away. It was just a glass.

"She had a blood clot in her lung, which is also called a thrombus," Nate started, and the story went from there.

The cemetery roadways were narrow and our mother drove slowly in case a car came from the other way, which it almost never did. The grass was neatly mowed. Any fresh mounds of dirt were covered with strips of bright green sod, making it look like the newer graves had more life in them. Some of the headstones, usually the ones with carvings of angels or inset pictures of Jesus, even pictures of the person who died, had lots of flowers around them. There were carnations in sturdy vases and votive candles everywhere. Our mother told us that people paid extra to have the cemetery staff come and leave those things once a month, once a week, if you really wanted to, but she said it didn't matter how many flowers there were, it was the love you left that was important. "Cemetery workers are paid to care," she shrugged. "Dead people may be dead, but they can still tell the difference. Not that we're judging."

We parked the car and Nate got the beach towel out of the trunk. The ground was a little soft and our mother's high heels sunk into the grass, kicking up lopsided cones of dirt as we headed over to our father's grave. She started walking on the balls of her feet, knees bent. "God," she said,

"I feel like a praying mantis." She took off her shoes and hooked one finger into each heel, the toes dangling.

"Praying mantises eat each other when they mate," Nate said.

"Actually, that's not true." My mother tapped the toes of her shoes together. "They only do that in laboratories when people are watching."

"But we saw them do it in the wild, on TV," I said.

"Well, somebody had to be holding the camera, don't you think?"

I helped Nate spread the beach towel lengthwise over our father's grave. It was yellow and it showed a hot pink flamingo wearing pineapple-shaped sunglasses. Our mother bought it on sale. She said that most people probably found it a bit loud, even for the beach, but that's what the graveyard needed, wasn't it? A little colour. "How would you like to live with only grey furniture?" she asked us, pointing at the gravestones. But it didn't really matter. All the towel had to do was keep our graveyard clothes clean.

Our father's name was carved into a large polished piece of granite, and then below that it said, "Son, Husband, Father, Caregiver." When Nate was younger, he had asked our mother if our father worked in schools or office buildings.

"That's a caretaker, Nate. A janitor. Your father was a doctor."

"So why couldn't he make himself better?"

"Why can't pigs fly?"

"They're mammals."

"So was your dad."

When Nate and I were done smoothing out the towel, my mother laid out a framed picture of us as a family, me in my mother's arms and Nate teetering on one tiny running shoe with his fists around my father's fingers. Beside that she stacked some oatmeal chocolate chip cookies. She thought the game worked better if we didn't have low blood sugar. She brushed the dirt off the bottoms of her bare feet and tied her hair back with an elastic band. "Okay, who wants to go first this time?"

The game wasn't the kind that Nate and I played with our friends. The kids we hung out with were mostly into four-square and dodge ball and a kind of football that we made up and called Astronaut. Those games had a winner and rules, teams, but the Dead Dad Game didn't have any of that. All we did was lie very still on the beach towel and listen, and to make our mother happy we sometimes made things up when she asked us, "What do you hear?" In a lot of ways it wasn't a game at all, but there was nothing else to call it. My mother said it was a game. It was just something we did.

"Nate, why don't you go?" My mother passed him a cookie. "Take your shoes off before you get on the towel."

Nate undid the laces of his stiff black shoes and lined them up beside my mother's high heels. He sat down and took a few deep breaths. My mother and I moved closer, perching on the edge of the towel to save our skirts, and Nate closed his eyes. My mother held out her hand to me and then we each took one of Nate's hands in ours, closing the circle. He wriggled in his suit.

"Wouldn't it be better if we just wore regular clothes?" I asked.

"It's more respectful this way." My mother squeezed our hands. "And people won't bug us as much if it looks like we came from a church. Now let's be quiet so Nate can listen."

My mother said that when bodies broke down and turned into grass and soil, there were vibrations. That's all that talking was, vibrations, so being dead didn't mean that you stopped talking, even if it wasn't in the same language. Nate had asked his Science Club teacher what she thought about that, and she said she hadn't heard the theory before, but there were a lot of things that still needed to be discovered in the world. That was the point of the club. Nate was convinced, or said he was.

"I hear," he paused, "I hear humming."

"That makes sense," my mother said slowly, but I didn't think it made sense at all. Why would our dad's body be humming? Was there that much to hum about when you were dead? Maybe he was just happy to see us, I thought. That was possible. Or maybe Nate was faking. That was possible, too. I faked.

"Can I have a cookie?" I asked.

"In a minute, Elaine." my mother said. "What else do you hear?"

The three of us closed our eyes and listened hard. I saw our father's vibrations crawling up like earthworms, tickling Nate's back with secret messages about how much he missed us, about the things that had made him afraid and sick. Our mother said that visualization was an important part of the game, and she always seemed to hear things, grunts or mumbles. I just needed to visualize harder, and then I would hear it too. Faking wasn't lying, it was practicing. Nate was about to say something else, but we heard a car door slam. We dropped our hands and opened our eyes.

It was the red cemetery maintenance truck. Two guys in matching windbreakers and baseball hats were fishing around in the flatbed. One of them grabbed a rake, and the other one hugged a giant bag of garden fertilizer.

"Shit," my mother said, and the game was over.

Nate balled up the towel and shoved it under his arm. He squashed his feet into his shoes, breaking down the backs. My mother shook out her hair. I packed the picture and cookies into her purse. My mother waved to the men as she hustled us to the car, and the one man raised his rake to us while the other one slit the fertilizer bag with a packing knife. We didn't play the game while other people watched. It didn't work that way, and there had been problems before. My mother told us that a lot of people have pretty un-evolved ideas about things. She had written letters to the cemetery's managing director about the behaviour of his employees.

"Let's not worry about it too much," she said, pushing play on the stereo. "It's not like your dad won't be here next Sunday. Seatbelts." We drove past Genevieve's grave on the way out. Nate waved.

We were almost home before I asked about the humming. My mother said that the whole universe hummed, that if we heard everybody's heartbeats, all at once, it would sound like the buzzing of a beehive. "We're all connected," she said.

"But what if you don't have a heartbeat?" I asked. "What about all the dead people?"

"I watched a show about bees," Nate said. "If you put a box of them in the freezer, they clump around the queen to keep her warm. After a few hours, you have this pile of dead bees."

"Were they killer bees?" my mother said. "Good hygiene is as important as a clear conscience."

My mother spun the steering wheel with the flat of one hand and leaned over to pop out the Stevie Wonder tape as we turned into our driveway. Nate was already unbuckling his seatbelt when my mother—"Oh shit," she said—swerved and jammed the brakes. The car lurched, hard, and Nate slammed into the back of the passenger seat. There was the hollow thud of metal hitting something softer than itself, and then right away a kind of shriek that at first I thought was Nate, and then I thought was my mother, my mother who wasn't like any other mother, no matter what Nate said, but then the shriek came again, from outside the car, again and again, until it died away and became softer, deeper, more like a humming.

"Oh shit," my mother said again. She took the keys out of the ignition. We got out of the car.

It wasn't actually a hum at all, once we heard it better. It was more of a phlegmy growl, a snuffling, and it was so steady that it didn't seem to matter if Mickey was breathing in or breathing out, and for a second I didn't think she was doing either. Her back legs were bent towards her tail and her feet were bleeding. Part of one leg was skinned. The muscle was pink and twitchy and looked like the kind of thing my mother refused to buy in chain grocery stores. Our front bumper was fine, but there was a strip of skin hanging underneath the car.

"Nate, get the toboggan," my mother said calmly, bending down and stroking Mickey's head with two fingers. But Nate stood there, fiddling with the car door handle, staring at Mickey as she groaned and licked my mother's wrist. "Nate." He slammed the door and took off for the garage. "Elaine, get the towel out of the trunk."

Nate ran with the toboggan scraping behind him on the asphalt. We lined it up beside Mickey and I laid the towel out over its wooden slats. My mother grabbed Mickey around the chest and hauled her up, letting her legs hang. "Jesus," she said, doing a power squat. Mickey shook as my mother lowered her onto the toboggan. Mickey's tongue hung out of her mouth. She was shivering and panting. I wrapped her in the towel and her legs felt like bags of loose marbles. The blood leaked through the pink flamingo and turned it orange.

My mother dragged the toboggan to Mr. Crisander's and Nate and I walked beside, each of us with a steadying hand on Mickey to make sure she didn't fall off. Mickey made squeaking noises when we tried to tilt the toboggan up the steps, and we decided that was a bad idea. My mother went up on the porch to ring the doorbell and I sat beside Mickey, keeping her company and whispering in her ear that she was a good girl, such a good girl, while she pawed at my arm with one of her front hooves. Nate got a stick and went back to the car. He started poking gently at the swinging skin. My mother rang the doorbell again and we waited. Then she knocked.

"If he's not home," she said, "we're going to have to take care of this ourselves." She watched me stroke gently under Mickey's chin with one finger. "Look at her."

I patted Mickey, pressing on her chest softly until I felt the fluttering of her heart and she let out a little grunt. This was taking care of her, I thought, wrapping her in a beach towel and keeping her warm so she might stop shivering.

"Elaine."

I was never going to let her go.

Mr. Crisander opened the door with an apron on and a checkered dish towel over one shoulder. His house smelled like burnt sugar. He patted his belly happily when he saw my mother.

"Natalie, I was ju—" His eyes flicked down to me and Mickey and he stopped. His mouth kept moving but I didn't understand the words that came out. He held his arms out and Mickey snuffled, closing her eyes. The towel was soaked. The words from Mr. Crisander turned into something that sounded like, "Mickey Mick-Mick, Mickey Mick-Mick," and he said it over and over as he drifted down the stairs with his arms out to her, like I was invisible and it was just Mickey he saw, begging for him to hold onto her before she disappeared like a dream he didn't remember. I draped one arm over Mickey and hugged her close.

"Elaine," my mother said again, more sharply. Mr. Crisander's arms kept gliding towards me, saying, "Mickey, Mick-Mick," until I felt Mickey shift under me. She made a noise that was almost a honk as Mr. Crisander picked her up. He moved effortlessly, like Mickey weighed nothing at all. He climbed the stairs and went inside without saying anything to us.

"John," my mother started, "if there's something—" but the door was already closed. Nate crouched by the tire. My cemetery blouse had pig blood on it, and my mother held her arms out in front of her, her wrists limp.

"Let's go wash our hands," she said.

It was a surprise to all of us that Mickey didn't die. She was back a few days later, lying in the bay window of Mr. Crisander's living room on a new and very plush white bed. Her back end was wrapped in gauze and an adult diaper with a hole cut out for her tail. Mr. Crisander changed her diaper every few hours, and it must have hurt her for him to do it; as soon as he started to unfasten the sticky tabs at the sides, Mickey's mouth opened and closed and we knew she was crying. My mother told us that she heard Mr. Crisander had taken a leave of absence from his job at the Veterans' Hospital. She tried phoning him, but he hung up as soon as she said, "John, it's Natalie." Nate and I left cards on the front porch, addressed to Mickey, but we saw them unopened in the recycling bin on garbage day. Mr. Crisander fed Mickey with a dinner spoon out of a large bowl and gave her water with an eye dropper. They did that for weeks, but Mickey's legs didn't seem to get any better.

On weekends Nate and I sat on the sidewalk outside Mr. Crisander's house and watched Mickey blink at us erratically. Sometimes we blinked back. Mickey didn't seem all that bad, we said. My mother agreed. "Some of the patchier parts of her skin look better," she noticed when she came to get us for dinner. Mr. Crisander ignored us, but he talked to Mickey a lot. Sometimes he turned her bed around so she was able to see the television while he watched old westerns. He even hung a cat toy from the ceiling for her, and Mickey batted it around and looked happy.

It was July before Mr. Crisander let us apologize. We were playing outside his house in our cemetery clothes. The sidewalk was cool, even though the sun was starting to steam the dew off the brown grass. It was getting hot and soon it would be scorching. Our mother was going to stripe our noses with neon green zinc, no matter what we had to say about it. If we didn't want skin cancer, she said, we were just going to have to put up with looking like idiots once in a while.

Nate leaned back on his elbows and watched Mickey blink. I drew pictures of pigs with sidewalk chalk. I made dozens of Mickeys, some with legs and some without, but all of them with big smiles on their faces and little noise lines coming off of them like they were alarm clocks. I was working on a very large and purple Mickey when Nate tapped my arm with his foot.

"Elaine," he said. "He's looking."

Mr. Crisander stood in the window and crossed his arms. He was wearing a bathrobe, and he had Mickey's bowl in one of his hands. Mickey was stretching her leg out at the food, but Mr. Crisander just kept staring at us. We had been waiting for this. We were sorry. My mother said that acceptance was the last stage of grief and we couldn't rush Mr. Crisander. We could only make offerings to him, and to Mickey. "Sidewalk chalk is good," she said. "If he's only made it as far as the anger stage and he flips out, I can just stretch the garden hose over. Sometimes guys like him flip out."

Nate and I stood up and waved to Mr. Crisander. He didn't wave back. Nate shouted, "Our thoughts are with you and Mickey at this difficult time." I pointed to the Mickeys on the sidewalk, their smiling faces like blue and green and purple suns, glowing, and their sound lines speaking to me: Hi, Elaine. I see you.

Mr. Crisander drew the curtains.

"Anger stage," Nate said.

I drew a few more chalk pigs and Nate watched the Mickey-shaped shadow behind the sheers. We were hopeful.

Mr. Crisander came out onto the porch. He had changed into bright blue jeans and a white t-shirt with sleeves that went past his elbows. He started for the sidewalk. Nate buttoned his suit jacket and I brushed the chalk off my hands. Mr. Crisander stood on his lawn and studied the upside down chalk Mickeys.

"Do you know where pigs like Mickey come from?" he asked.

We didn't.

"Vietnam," he said. His eyes paused on the giant purple Mickey. "My son lives there."

"You have a son?" Nate was surprised. Mr. Crisander was terrible at baseball. "What's he doing in Vietnam?"

"Does Mickey ever get homesick?" I asked.

"Let's have some Kool-Aid." Mr. Crisander said. "Mickey misses you two."

We had never been inside Mr. Crisander's house before. My mother drove us to and from the baseball games and sat in the stands and read a magazine. She said that the baseball diamond was one thing but a person's house was another. If Mr. Crisander ever invited us in, we were supposed to check with her first. "All I'm saying is, better safe than on Geraldo," she said. But Mr. Crisander had never asked before and he might not ask again. Nate and I wanted to see Mickey. We followed him up the front walk.

His house was the same as ours—the living room was to the left of the front door, and on the other side there were twisty stairs to the basement, and down the middle, a hallway that led to the kitchen—but Mr. Crisander's house seemed bigger because it was so empty. In our living room we had a sofa that turned into a bed, a loveseat, a bookshelf, and a big coffee table that my mother buffed with Pledge before my aunts came over. Mr. Crisander only had a rabbit ear TV and a VCR, and an olive green wingback chair that was rubbed down to beige on one side. Mickey blinked at us from her bed in the window seat.

"Look who's here, Mickey," Mr. Crisander said loudly. We stood in the alcove and waved. Mickey blinked back.

"She's doing a lot better," Mr. Crisander said more softly to us. "But the vet says she's a little heavy from the lack of exercise. I'm thinking of making her a wheelchair she can power with her front legs."

Mickey's front legs looked like spindly little toothpicks that had been jammed into her giant watermelon body, but we didn't say anything.

"We'll be in the kitchen if you need us, Mickey," Mr. Crisander shouted. "Her hearing's going," he said as we walked down the hallway.

Mr. Crisander dumped two packets of Kool-Aid powder into a big blue pitcher, but he filled it to the brim without even measuring and he didn't stir for long enough. The Kool-Aid tasted like water but looked like pale blood.

"Would you like to see Mickey's room?" he asked.

"Mickey has her own room?" I couldn't believe it. Mickey was the luckiest pig in the world.

"We have bunk beds," Nate said as Mr. Crisander took us back down the hall.

"Well, pigs aren't very good with ladders," he said.

Mickey's room was painted light purple. She had a wooden scratching post drilled into the floor and a large rope with big knots that was probably a toy. There was a giant teddy bear losing his stuffing from a hole in his face, and a beanbag chair with a Mickey-sized depression still in the middle of it. In the corner of the room there was a large doghouse in the shape of an igloo. Inside it we saw a fluffy pink comforter. Mickey also had a radio. It was set high on a wooden shelf near the top of the window, and it was tuned to the same station my mother liked.

"What do you think?"

Next to the radio was a small picture in a gold frame. The photo was blurry and old, the corners of it yellow and blotchy. It was even harder to see because it was up so high, but we could tell it was of a woman with long dark hair and tiny eyes. She wore a funny-looking pointed hat that cast a big shadow over her face, but I still saw that she had a hand over her mouth. She might have been smiling.

"Is that your wife?" Nate pointed. Suddenly it seemed possible that someone like Mr. Crisander might have a wife.

"No," Mr. Crisander said, "she's not."

Nate and I finished our drinks. "Thanks for the Kool-Aid. It was really good," I lied.

Mr. Crisander told us we were welcome any time we liked. Any friend of Mickey's was a friend of his, and bygones were bygones.

"Maybe on Friday night you guys can come over and watch a movie," he said as we made our way to the front door. "Give your mom a break. I'll make popcorn."

Maybe, we said, but right now we had to go. It was Sunday and we were already late.

POSES

YEAH, ALICE WILL DO IT, I'M SURE. She's always ready to do anything I say, just sometimes she makes me go first. Like one time I asked her if she wanted to look at my dad's magazines, the ones he keeps in the firebox. Which is kind of a weird place to keep them, I think, because they get all full of wood shavings and stuff and then mice pee on them and I'm like, Dad, hello, learn how to turn on the computer, why don't you? But whatever, maybe these are what he likes. Women with retro haircuts and furry beavs wearing high heels and making cupcakes. Still, like you couldn't find that on Google. But the point is that Alice was all like, Sure, I'll do it, whatever, but it was my idea and Alice made me open the box.

There was a picture of this woman sitting on a bed with her legs open. And I mean wide open. She had her fingers down there, like she was checking to make sure that everything was in the right place, or something, but her eyes were looking off into the top right corner of the room in a way that made you wonder what she was thinking about. Maybe something like, Is my dentist appointment on Tuesday or Thursday? or What time did that pot roast go in the oven? Touching herself the whole time like the answers were in her hoo-ha, which is the word my mom uses instead of vagina. Lauren, she'll say to me in the summer, you should get out of that wet bathing suit before you rot your hoo-ha. I don't know why, but all I can picture when she says that is a big hot air balloon full of mould. Go figure, but it makes me put on underwear.

The woman on the bed had her mouth open, not in a smile, but you still saw her teeth, white like she'd never puckered up to anything but bright clean sunshine. Really you know that no amount of Colgate or Ivory or even Javex will ever get that mouth clean. Which is the point, obviously.

Alice said, Doesn't your mom get mad about these?

I thought about that. I tried to imagine my dad taking the old Leica off the shelf in the bedroom closet and saying, Okay, Karen. Sit on the edge of the bed. Spread your legs. Yep, be more pinchy with your fingernails. Now, look at the corner of the ceiling like you're trying to decide which of the kids' Halloween costumes to sew next. And my mom, purple spider veins on her thighs, holding the pose like she was sitting for one of those oldie timey photographs you can get at Pioneer Village, saying through her closed teeth, Are you almost done, Eric? I think the dishwasher's finished and I don't want spots.

No, I said to Alice. I bet she probably doesn't mind. And Alice said, Well, I would. Who'd want her husband looking at pictures of other girls' you-knows. And I was like, What, hoo-has? Snatches? Twats? But Alice gave me this look and said, God, Lauren. Sometimes you don't know when to quit.

I get that a lot.

Sorry, my arm is tired. Okay, I'm good.

Yeah, Mrs. Ogilvy said those exact words to me, except for the part about God, because I don't think you're allowed to talk about God at school anymore. Not like when my mom went to school and they made her pray before every math test and spelling bee, and do creepy stuff like kiss her crucifix before trying to jump over the pommel horse in gym. But then again, what do you expect when you go to Our Lady of Perpetual Sorrow and all your teachers are named Sister Mary Jehosephat, or whatever? So Mrs. Ogilvy didn't say God, because I don't go to a Catholic school, and because if anyone's got a pickle up her bum about what you're allowed and not allowed to do it's Mrs. Ogilvy, but she definitely said, Lauren, sometimes you don't know when to quit.

She said it because I did this thing that I do sometimes, this thing where I fall over. I've perfected my technique so it looks really painful, but it isn't. I roll my eyes back in my head so people can only see the white parts, and then I twist my lips up into this weird kind of face. I've learned to keep my mouth closed and my teeth clenched so I don't bite my tongue. Then I click my shoulder blade out of place—I'm double-jointed—and jerk my shoulder up to my ear. After about a half-second I let one side of my body, I'm better at the left side, go limp and I just kind of crumple in on myself. Blam. I jerk my left arm up at the elbow in kind of a spastic way when I do it, so it looks like maybe I'm having a seizure or a stroke, or something, but really it's for balance. It's a controlled fall.

I got the idea from reading this book by a girl with epilepsy. The girl had to go to this special school for epileptics that was run by nuns, and one of the things the nuns taught them to do was fall. That way if the girls felt a seizure coming on, they could fall on their own time and be on the ground when it came, and they wouldn't seize standing up and crack their heads open. I don't know how the nuns knew what they were talking about. I mean, they were nuns, not physiotherapists, right? But their training methods made sense. First they got the girls—they were all girls—to fall into a swimming pool, so they could get used to the feeling of falling, the loss of gravity, and stuff. Then they made them practice the same sort of thing but on these cushy gym mats. The girl in the story described the process in very poetic terms. She wrote that the girls in the water were like spreading lilies and that the girls on the mats were like drifting snowflakes, and all of that. It was cool to read but not all that helpful when it came to learning how to fall, especially because I don't have a pool or a cushy gym mat and so I had to start with my bed, which was okay, and then move on to thick basement carpet, which gave me rug burn.

Eventually I got it, though. At first Alice thought it was stupid, but then I showed her that it's actually pretty crazy. Like I said, sometimes I just have to do stuff first.

I used it at this variety store across the street from the school. The man behind the counter is an Indian guy with a turban. He's got this weird rolled-up twist of hair that comes out from the turban on one side, goes under his chin and then gets tucked up into the turban on the other side. It kind of supports his double chin. I know that's not the reason behind it, but it seems sort of rude to ask, Hey, what's with that hair strap that you've got under your chin? So I just let it go. I went in there one day and asked him for a pack of cigarettes.

Belmont Lights, I said, leaning on the counter in front of the candy bars and trying to play it cool. Like maybe if he noticed that I wasn't staring at his hair strap, he wouldn't give me a hard time about the cigarettes. They're for my mom, I said, pointing across the street to a car that had a bored-looking woman in it. The woman was checking her watch and flipping her hair in the rear-view mirror, putting on lipstick and drinking a coffee, all at once. She looked like the type who sent her daughter for cigarettes, I thought, but the guy hesitated. He looked at me like maybe I was just another punk kid trying to shove jawbreakers in my pocket when he turned his back, which, for the record, is not the kind of person I am at all. I had already calculated the exact change for the cigarettes. So I decided to fall.

I rolled back my eyes and twisted my mouth and twitched my shoulder and then did the arm thing. Blam, there I was on the floor in front of the counter, a few chocolate bars spilling off the shelves, and the guy looking like he was going to crap his pants because now he had a dead girl in his store. I got up quickly and was all like, Sorry, sorry. My mom . . . I need to go. I acted all embarrassed and apologetic and scared, like my mom, waiting in the car and plucking her eyebrows, was going to beat me if I was five minutes late with her cigarettes. Like maybe I was subject to all kinds of nic-fit beatings and that's why I had the falling problem. I don't know what he thought, but he gave me the cigarettes and hustled me out of the store. I'm a really good actress.

From then on, I'd just walk into the store and he'd have a pack of Belmonts in his hand like that, like the faster he sold me the cigarettes, the less chance there was of me falling and dying in his store and clogging up the aisles that were already jammed with kids who were trying to tuck porno magazines into the sleeves of their jackets. He had enough to deal with, I guess, so it was just easier to sell the cigarettes to the girl with the exact change and the freaky falling problem and not question it. It worked out well.

One time, though, the regular guy wasn't there. It was some young dude in a homemade t-shirt that said Sikh and Destroy on it. For a second I thought he might be cool with just selling me the cigarettes right off, but then I thought I'd better do the falling thing, just to be safe. But because I was out of practice, I actually hit my head on this giant Doublemint gum cardboard display and gave myself a little cut. It wasn't a big deal. Anyone who has taken the St. John Ambulance babysitting course knows that head wounds can really gush and it's usually not something to go ape about. Evidently this guy hadn't taken the course and he completely freaked out. He ran out of the store, shouting for an ambulance, a doctor, the police, you name it. It was kind of ridiculous. There he is trying to be all tough and religious in his Sikh and Destroy shirt and he's crying and waving his arms because a twelve-year-old girl knocked over a gum display thing. I tried to shout at him that I was fine, to never mind about the cigarettes, but by that time there were people running down the street towards the store. Even the crossing guard man who has Down's Syndrome was coming over to see what was wrong. Seriously.

Mrs. Ogilvy was on bus duty that day and she was the first one there from the school. Mouth open, she saw my bleeding forehead and the whole smashed up Doublemint display. She leaned forward, moving her whole body back and forth like she was one of those drinking bird toys. That's when she said it: Lauren, sometimes you don't know when to quit. You almost felt like the words *For God's sake* were on her tongue, but they never came out, even though I suppose we weren't technically at school and so it was fine to mention God.

No, it doesn't hurt. I told you, I'm double-jointed. And I don't have to be home until five.

My sister is the quitter. Ballet, gymnastics, floor hockey, piano, guitar, high school. Whatever. Sometimes when people, mostly people like old Girl Guide leaders, the ones with pleated pants and dumpy bums, run into her at the grocery store where she works, they'll ask her what she's planning to do in the fall. Get pregnant, maybe, she says. Or drunk. There have been lots of complaints to the deli manager. She wears midnight blue eyeliner and black and white striped arm warmers that she cut thumbholes into, even though we're all like, Um, hi, but it's twenty-seven degrees outside and your elbows have a rash from the wool that sat in some hobo-infested donation bin for the past six months. But when she's working she has to take them off so she doesn't contaminate the meat, thank God, and instead she wears an XXL polo shirt that says Food Giant in fluorescent yellow letters. She has to roll up the sleeves of the t-shirt six times so they don't get sucked into the meat slicing machines. My mom says it's a safety hazard. My sister also has to wear steel-toed work boots that she says make her look like a dyke, and a nametag, so people know who to complain about. Her name is Margot.

Margot was a vegetarian for a while. Really she was on some crazy crash diet and not eating, period, but the meat thing was her excuse. Everything my mother cooked had come into contact with meat, or animal fat, or honey from exploited bees, or something, and so Margot was able to hide her whole no-food diet thing until she got anemic and started fainting at work.

I refuse to eat lips and assholes, was what she said when my mom barbecued hotdogs. I kiss enough ass as it is at the store.

You and everyone else, my mother said above the sizzle of wiener fat. But get used to it, Margot, the whole world is one big behind. Now watch your language. Your sister's here, and we have company.

But the company we had was just Alice. My mom thinks that because Alice always says please and thank you and doesn't push her peas onto her fork with her finger that she's some kind of angel child, and that hearing a swear word might tarnish the glow of her halo, or something. But who do you think I smoke those Belmonts with? Alice is actually the one who taught me how to smoke and told me that it helps keep you skinny. She learned from her grandma who has emphysema. She knows what she's doing.

And that's the thing. I didn't mean to make Alice sound like this priss and me like this jerk who falls on the ground to get what she wants. It's actually not like that. Alice only does things that she wants to do, and she's not an idiot. Like if some bozo in a white van asked her to help him find his lost puppy, she'd tell him where to go, and scream bloody murder if he tried anything. She knows a pervert when she sees one, no offense. And when we took that self-defence class, Alice was the best at it. She kicked the guy in the balls.

Oh yeah, she did. The girls in grade six had to go to the gym for this class every Monday for about a month. This female cop came to lead a seminar called I Am Not a Victim that mostly seemed to be about my bum falling asleep on the gym floor while we watched videos about girls in miniskirts sneaking off to lame parties where guys with pimples gave them spiked drinks. The girls were always named Tiffany or

Crystal, or something, I don't know what that was about. They drank the booze and then got raped off camera. More often, though, they just almost got raped and then had to run home through an alleyway to their moms who made them tea and told them they were proud that they hadn't been a victim. I don't know what planet these videos are made on, but if I came home at three in the morning looking like an extra from *In Living Colour* and stinking of booze, my mom would have a conniption, and for once it'd be me, not Margot, who was going to send my dad to an early grave.

The cop also made us do these weird partner exercises, which I was glad of because at least they brought my ass back to the land of the living. Alice was my partner. For this one, Alice was supposed to close her eyes and I was supposed to walk towards her, and when Alice felt that her personal space was invaded, or whatever, she was supposed to put one hand out in front of her and say, Please back up. You're in my personal space. It was supposed to make us assertive about the rights of our bodies, or something. I forget exactly, now. But the point is that when we did it I just kept walking closer and closer to Alice until our noses were practically touching, and she didn't say anything. Finally I was so close that I could smell her skin, the heat of it, I mean, and I was like, Alice, am I invading your space yet or what? She just shrugged, her eyes closed and said, I know it's you.

About halfway through the last class we had this guy come in all covered in foam and hockey kind of equipment and a mask, and he was this make-believe attacker. We were supposed to go up one at a time and scream in his face *I am not a victim!* in order to empower ourselves. If we wanted to, we could kick him in the crotch, and, just in case we didn't know where his crotch was, like if we'd been sleeping through all those date rape videos, or something, he was wearing this big bull's eye on a kind of paper plate thing between his legs. Alice was the only one who did it. Who kicked him, I mean. I didn't do it because I thought it must be a pretty crappy job to have to come to a gym and get kicked in the balls by fifty sixth-grade girls, no matter what kind of gear you're wearing. He's probably some junior cop trainee and this job, which they say is part of serving the community, is actually new-cop hazing, and everybody at the station is snickering when he comes in the next day and has to sit at his desk with an ice pack on his junk. But Alice did it.

She walked right up to him and looked him in the hockey mask and screamed *I am not a victim!* in a voice that gave me the shivers. Seriously. Then she wound up her foot like she was a cartoon donkey, or something, and totally socked him. I mean, the guy is wearing his paper plate shield and a jock and foam and who knows what else, and he actually crumples to his knees. The female cop was all like, Uh, well done, oh-kay, but you could tell she hadn't been expecting that one. It's funny, right? You could tell that on the one hand she was proud of herself, like she'd taught us Krav Maga, or something, and on the other she was worried, like, What have I done here? But that's sort of the thing about Alice. She does that to you, once in a while.

What?

Yeah, right. Surprises you.

Some people think she's kind of a loser, or whatever, but she's totally not. She'd be cool. I mean, she's not as mature as me about this kind of stuff, obviously, but I'd talk to her about it. I'd just tell her that I did it first and it'd be fine.

It's not like this stuff is any more slutty than what Margot wore in Cuba last year. She had this bikini that was the slut-

tiest thing I'd ever seen, honest to God. First of all, it was crocheted. And not crocheted like some Polish grandma spent
hours pulling the stitches tight, but totally loose so you
could see patches of skin. Wide weave, for sure. Her boobs
were hardly even covered, and it's not like she had a lot of
boobs then. She was just coming off the no-food diet and a
quarter would have covered things up. I don't even know
what would have happened if she'd got it wet because when
she came out of the hotel and started walking to the beach,
my dad freaked and smothered her in his beach towel like
she was on fire or something, and Margot started screaming
that he was trying to oppress her. It was wild.

Everyone at the hotel beach bar was totally on Margot's
side. Think about it: you're at the beach when all of a sudden
a girl in a skanky bikini is screaming for your help because
some fat dude is wrestling her to the ground. What do you
do? These Brazilian guys who didn't speak English ran up
and tried to pry them apart, and my dad kept saying, She's
my daughter, she's my daughter, but who knows what that
sounds like in Brazilian or whatever, and so one of the guys
punched him in the face and broke his nose. There was
blood everywhere. Seriously. There was a bunch of screaming and crying and my mother kept saying, You've ruined
Christmas, you've ruined Christmas, but it was hard to know
who she was saying it to. Probably Margot, because Margot
has a habit of ruining everything. After that the hotel people
hated us because they had to close the pool to clean out the
blood that got sprayed in there. And Margot bought that
bikini at The Bay. I mean, get over it.

If I were Margot, I'd have a plan. I mean, what is she
going to do, spend her life at Food Giant watching old ladies
cruise the aisles for Depends? Whatever. Maybe that's why

she was trying to starve herself to death. Her life was just too depressing to put another Pop-Tart in her mouth. I don't know. But I can tell you that by the time I'm seventeen, I'm not going to be slicing salami for picky moms in stretch pants. I'm going to move to New York, or L.A., or just someplace where people don't get excited about the new roof on the community centre. I'll get a job in a restaurant and write postcards home so my parents don't flip: Hi Mom. Alphabet City is nice. The local Welcome Wagon brought me a Brie wheel. Whatever. That's what I'm saving for now. I even quit smoking. It's too expensive.

So I think, what do I care if a bunch of nerds see these? It's not like that does anything to me. I'm not an idiot. I know what I'm doing. And yeah, Alice will totally do it too. I'm her best friend. She trusts me. But the point is your ad said that if I brought in another girl I'd get paid more, and you never said how much.

Hurricane SEASON

MAIRIN WAS ON HOLIDAY, in the strictest sense of the word. The sense in which she was entitled to wear oversized sunglasses and red toenail polish, a black head scarf, should the wind prove too much for her pale blonde curls. She was trying not to think about the missed appointment, because that's what holidays were for, weren't they? Trading hard decisions for simple ones. What would you like? José the bartender had asked her on the first day as she dangled her painted toes in the pool, legs covered in goosebumps. Rum and Coke, please, she said after a moment, and within seconds, ta da—breakfast. The efficiency both startled and pleased her; it was so easy to get exactly what she wanted.

And that was why people came. For the sun, the sand, the cheap drinks mixed by attractive, dark-skinned men who smiled and said, *De nada* when you thanked them. They didn't come for these unseasonably cool temperatures and an ocean that washed dead fish and bottles onto the beach.

It's colder than it should be for the time of year, José said every morning to the pale tourists in their windbreakers. I'm sorry.

Mairin had brought only one sweater with her, a three-quarter sleeve black cardigan with iridescent buttons. You won't need more than this, her mother had said, folding it gently into the American Tourister suitcase. You just throw it on over a sundress and no problem! Mairin, wearing the sweater over her new blue and green bikini, shivered. She leaned back onto the deck chair and let the plastic webbing gently bite the fleshiness of her thighs. She put on her sunglasses to stare at the overcast sky, unobserved.

Mairin had spent a lot of time at the pool over the past ten days, long enough to make a habit of having a drink when José started his shift at ten each morning, and to find out that he had a wife and two little girls. Oh, Mairin had said, yes, she would like to see a picture, and José had taken the creased paper out of his breast pocket and smoothed it out on the bar with careful fingers.

"Maria," he had said, pointing to the smaller girl whose face was mostly covered by a thumb-sucking fist. "And Pené-lope," he pointed again, the girl frowning, her face slightly turned away from the camera as though someone had unexpectedly called her name.

"They're beautiful," Mairin said.

"Like their mother." José refolded the photo and put it into his pocket. "Isabella. And you?"

"No," Mairin said. "No kids."

By the early afternoon she often found herself drunk and sleepy, teetering back to her room, fingers brushing against the rough bark of palm trees. Every day the maids gave her new towels that smelled of bleach. They folded them into swans. Two swans, kissing, with flowers in their towel-beaks. If Mairin was very drunk, she put the flowers in her hair and smoothed the towels over herself, dreaming of clean, white, disinfected beaches. She made a point of showering and dressing for dinner, even though she dreaded the American-style pulled pork she endured sitting beside the fat German who was perpetually sunburned despite the weather, who chewed with his mouth open and said, tiny pieces of pork flying towards her, Mairin, you are very beautiful. After dinner she escaped to the beach, walking through the rain with her sandals in her hand, dehydrated, smelling of meat, make-up washing from her skin. Later she fell asleep under the towels on her bed thinking, The End, as though she were a character in a tremendously boring film noir. There was already some comfort in the routine.

But right now the beach chair was biting harder, the webbing probably leaving red marks on her skin. Her cue for another drink. Don't be sloppy, Mairin told herself as she strolled towards the bar. Sloppiness, her mother said, is the sure sign of a tart, and a real lady acts like a cupcake, not a tart.

"Rum and Coke, please, José," Mairin said as sweetly as possible. And suddenly there was the glass in her hand. Easy.

If only it were sunny. Her mother had told her to get a tan.

"Men don't like pasty-faced girls, Mair," she had said at the airport. "You need to relax in the sun, get some colour. You look tired." She hooked a thumb in the direction of a kissing couple at the taxi stand. "Maybe if you didn't look so tired, you wouldn't need your mother to see you off."

"I don't need you to," Mairin had said.

"Oh, come on now." She pushed some hair behind Mairin's ear. "You look just like Mary Tyler Moore, only with better hair. Don't worry, you'll find someone."

The airport hummed with the sounds of families snaking their way to check-in desks, trying to sweep their lolling children off the floor, saying in brittle voices, Hold Mummy's hand.

"See?" her mother said. "I told you six o'clock wasn't too early. You young girls are all the same—you think the world will wait for you if you're twenty minutes late. But it won't, and don't you forget it."

The check-in line shuffled forward.

"This'll be good for you," her mother said, patting her hand. "You just need a break, a change of pace to get you out of the funk you're in these days."

"I'm not in a funk," Mairin said.

The line moved again.

"I'm your mother, Mairin. Not an idiot."

"Next, please," the ticket agent said.

The agent was thin in a way that made Mairin uncomfortable. Her eyes seemed too big for her reddened eyelids. She had the appearance of an overworked racehorse.

"Yes," Mairin said, "I'm next."

The horse-faced woman eyed Mairin's large backpack.

"I'm going to have to ask you to check that bag, ma'am," she said mechanically, her large teeth catching her lips. "It's oversized." She offered a plastic baggie in which to carry anything medically or legally necessary for the duration of the flight—Mairin's wallet, her passport, eyeglasses, a new pack of birth control pills, her asthma inhaler, and a fistful of tampons.

"God, Mair," her mother said, eyeing the tampons. "It's only a five-hour trip."

"Thank you," Mairin said to the ticket agent as she took her boarding pass.

"Did you see that woman's face?" her mother asked as they walked over to the security checkpoint. "You'd think they'd put her in the back. On the telephone, or something."

"Gate eleven," Mairin said, speeding up.

Her mother held her elbow with two hands.

"I wish you'd tell me what's the matter," she said.

"I just need a vacation, like you said."

"Everyone needs a vacation. I'm talking about whatever it is that's been making you look so tired."

"Mom."

"Okay, don't tell me. And walk as fast as you want. Don't worry about my hip, which is getting worse, by the way, that's what Doctor Smolkin says, but you wouldn't know that because you don't even bother to talk to me anymore. Your own mother!"

Mairin gripped her baggie. "Mom, stop it."

Her mother planted herself with a rubber-soled squeak in the middle of the airport. She rubbed her hands up and down Mairin's arms.

"Oh fine. I know, I know. You go on, have a good time. Leave your crabby old mother behind and go find some nice man on the beach. We'll talk when you get back. Go on, go." She shooed Mairin like she would a pigeon.

Mairin walked under a sign printed in several languages: PASSENGERS ONLY BEYOND THIS POINT. She glanced back to see her mother exaggerating the up and down flap of her hand and straining her neck forward like an anxious turtle. It was the kind of wave she usually reserved for mentally disabled children she saw drooling in their wheelchairs on special education buses. See, Mairin, she would say reproachfully, waving as the children squealed and thrashed, even the retards make an effort.

Mairin waved back to her mother and then made her way through security and to the airport bar.

"Rum and Coke, please," she said to the bartender before being informed by the bored-looking man that he was not permitted to serve alcohol at that hour of the day. So Mairin had waited an hour on a hard plastic chair outside gate eleven, legs crossed, baggie in her lap, bleeding, she found out later, right through her jeans: "Excuse me," the woman behind her in line had whispered softly over the tinny sound of the final boarding call, "but I think you've had an accident."

She had since bled through the two bathing suits she had brought; the blue and green bikini was a purchase from the hotel gift shop. José had told her it was pretty, that the blue was the colour the ocean should be, that he was sorry, again, that it was so cold.

"That's okay," Mairin said. The program on the television behind the bar was interrupted by the local news station. The muted mouths of the news anchors opened and closed in foreign shapes that Mairin could not lip-read. "It's not your fault."

* * *

PEOPLE WERE LEAVING THE ISLAND any way they could. The fat German asked Mairin to come with him. He was flying to Toronto, then Berlin. Had she ever seen the Reichstag? he asked her seductively.

"I'm not that keen on empire," Mairin said, nailing plywood over one of the hotel dining room's ocean-facing windows. There were several more windows to do and the sky was already pale lilac. She imagined fish flying like birds into the glass. Starfish spinning deadly cartwheels of orange and purple. Palm fronds as giant whips, lashing.

"Maybe you are just playing hard to get," the German said, his hand on her arm.

"No," Mairin said, tapping one of his fingernails with her hammer, "I'm more playing hard to like."

Mairin helped organize the water and the canned food. She watched television with the hotel staff in the manager's stuffy office, José translating for her as though the picture of the swirling cloud, enhanced so as to appear pink on its edges, purple at its centre, wasn't enough information.

"They are saying it's early this year. Hurricane season. They are saying it's going to be bad."

"Yeah, José," Mairin said, sipping a rum and Coke, "I got that from the picture."

The travel agent who sold Mairin her plane ticket had shown her pictures of white beaches and children in snorkel gear. Of pineapples and smiling men and bikini-clad women. There had been no mention of hurricanes. The woman had simply punched Mairin's information into her computer with square, red fingernails and asked, deferentially batting her spidery eyelashes, would Mairin be travelling with a companion, which would qualify her for the couple's discount package?

"No," Mairin said, her legs crossed.

"Good for you," the travel agent said with conviction, her dangly earrings clanking with each head shake. "Young girls like you need to go out there and go a bit crazy." She shook her hands side to side when she said "crazy," as though it was a new kind of spastic dance.

"I guess so."

"And besides," the travel agent said quietly, eyeing the back of her supervisor's head, "the things I hear about Latin men. You wouldn't believe." She licked at the chocolate crust on her lip.

"Oh," Mairin said.

"Tracey, over there," the travel agent pointed to a young woman in a black turtleneck sweater, "she's gone down south on a couple of our promotions, and the things that come out of her mouth when she comes back." The travel agent looked at Mairin with conspiratorial prudery and then winked. "Let's just say it's nothing compared to what went in it."

Mairin shifted in her seat.

"If you don't mind, I'm in a bit of a rush."

"Well," the travel agent said, tossing back her blonde hair, "I see." She ignored Mairin for several moments while she clicked needlessly on her computer keyboard. Eventually she looked at Mairin again over the frame of her glasses. "And when would you like to travel?"

"Tomorrow," Mairin said.

"Tomorrow?" she blinked quickly, her fingers already typing. "That's lovely." She looked back at the screen. "I'm not sure there's going to be anything available so quickly. Are you sure you wouldn't want to wait a bit? We have some packages next month that are very reasonably priced."

"No," Mairin said, her hands folded in her lap. "It's tomorrow or nothing."

There was more typing, more blinking.

"Well, here's something, but the flight is very early in the morning. First thing."

"The plane will be cleaner."

The ticket came in an envelope that featured a picture of an aquamarine ocean, the word "Heaven" in elaborate script. Mairin had clutched the envelope during her flight, sweating until the ocean rippled and her hands were smudged with blue ink that no amount of scrubbing with pink airport bathroom soap would remove.

Her hands were still stained two weeks later as she and José stacked the chairs in the hotel dining room, tying them together, then to the support beams, José showing her the fisherman's knots he'd learned from his father.

"No, no, like this," José corrected, his hands on hers, the coarse rope between their fingers.

"Oh."

"You should really try to get that ink off your hands," he said, stopping to hold her hand and rub the ink stains with his thumbs. "I've heard it makes you sick. Gives you cancer."

Mairin packed six more peach floral seat cushions into wicker baskets and shrugged. "What doesn't these days?"

"You know," José said, "hurricanes are powerful storms." He stared out into the grey ocean, speaking to it before one of the cooks nailed a plywood board over the window. "People die in them."

"People die all the time, José."

"Maybe you should go. I could take you to the airport."

But they both knew that the wind had picked up. The rain had started.

"I'll take my chances," Mairin said, walking to the supply cupboard for another length of rope.

She had a chance, the specialist told her. After all, she was young and a non-smoker. She exercised, ate spinach, meditated. She avoided red meat and too much sun. Her mother, except for an arthritic hip, was in excellent health. Mairin did not use vaginal deodorants. She had never had a sexually transmitted disease. In many ways, the doctor had said as she lay bleeding very slowly on his examination table, she was an excellent candidate for aggressive treatment. She had nothing to lose.

"Thank you," Mairin said automatically.

"Absolutely excellent."

The doctor's voice came to Mairin from behind the pale green sheet a medical student had told her to drape over her thighs. She wondered what she looked like, the parts of her warmed by the incandescent bulb of the swing-armed lamp the doctor had turned on and angled low as he'd asked her to breathe out, relax a little. Mairin had turned her eyes to the ceiling, browned in the corner by some long-forgotten water damage, and focused on a picture from a magazine that someone, the kindly nurse, maybe, had taped there to distract people.

"We need to act quickly," the doctor was saying as he scraped a tissue sample from, it felt, the underside of Mairin's belly button. "I'll put a rush on these tests, and once they come back we'll be in a better position to consider your options." He looked at her and the glare from the lamp reflected white in his glasses, giving him the appearance of blindness. "And I want you to know you do have options. We'll discuss them tomorrow. I can fit you in very early, first thing."

Mairin looked at the picture on the ceiling. At the white sand like sugar that dissolved into the dark blues, then greens, then blue-blacks of the soft and nearly still ocean as the setting sun bled pink and orange into the water, the rivulets of light coursing slowly back to the deserted shore.

"Some new studies involving targeted radiation therapy have proven very encouraging," the doctor was saying. "Depending on these results, we may also want to consider chemotherapy. And there is the option of surgery." He scraped again. "I wouldn't normally recommend that for a woman your age. Have you thought about children?"

The palm tree was almost a silhouette against the ash-blue sky. The ripples on the water and the motion of the fronds made Mairin think unspoken words that rolled around on her tongue like glass bottles on the ocean, letters inside: *Tropic of Capricorn. Tropic of Cancer.*

"Yes," she said. "No."

Mairin shifted, her bum sticking to the sweaty paper sheet beneath her.

"Is the light getting a little warm?" the specialist had asked, swabbing.

Mairin, eyes on the picture, thought about lying on the beach at night and soaking in the sun as it leaked back out of each grain of sand.

"No," she had said. "It's great."

Mairin came back to the dining room in time to see José nail the last window shut.

"See, Mairin?" he said, knocking on the wood. "You're going to be fine."

*　　*　　*

MAIRIN WAS ALMOST ASLEEP, drunk and with a headache, on the floor of the manager's office. It was the only place in the hotel with a heavy wooden door and no windows. José had found her a pillow and a blanket and tucked her in beneath the manager's desk, telling her not to worry, that the storm was glancing off the east side of the island and would likely spin back out to the ocean. "You might get some time on the beach after all," he said, untwisting the bathing suit strap on her shoulder.

"I'm on holiday," Mairin slurred.

And she was. The carpet beneath her felt cool like silica, and the rattling fan in the corner sounded almost like the wind rustling in palm fronds. The underside of the plywood desk was her beach umbrella, her shelter from the sun, from the storm. She had stopped bleeding.

She felt like a child, taken care of and planned for. Her mother. Where was her mother? Her mother in a yellow dress, swearing in the kitchen as she tried to spell "Happy Birthday Mairin" in chocolate frosting. Multicoloured balloons and bean bag toss games, ribbons curled with the sharp edge of kitchen scissors, boys pushing other boys into girls who stood shyly in their party dresses and patent leather shoes, in tears. Palm trees, suddenly, in the backyard by the swing set, a lilac sky and rain. Her mother, shouting, Come on in, kids. You're gonna catch your deaths! And Mairin swinging higher and higher, tilting in the blackness of the afternoon, her head back as she pumped her legs and felt the rain spatter against the fire from her hot bones.

The wind split itself open. It became a mouth. It bit at her party dress and gnashed the shoes from her feet, hurtling them into the windows of the house. The sound of the glass breaking was lost in the swirling howl, but Mairin could hear the shards fly back at her, humming in the rain like exotic and deadly insects, stinging her bare arms and legs, her cheeks, making her bleed. A single piece of white-hot glass in her eye, another in her mouth, so that she saw white nothingness, so that when she tried to scream, a waterfall of white sand poured out of her.

The wind licked her hands away from the swing set chains and Mairin fell backwards into the ocean that appeared beneath her, the splinters from floating plywood boards finding ways into her fingertips, the sting of salt in her hands as she sank through the layers of water, dark blue, then green, then blue-black, until Mairin was numb, until she was frozen in her green and blue party dress at the bottom of the ocean like a small, beautiful stone.

She woke to the sound of the rattling fan. The rain had stopped and the birds—what happened to birds in a hurricane? Mairin wondered. Where did they go?—were silent. Mairin folded the blanket and fluffed the pillow that had creased her cheek and went to look for José. To return the bedding. To thank him for the rum and Cokes. To give him a hug. A hundred American dollars, maybe, if he would take it.

Mairin walked through the dark hotel. Plywood covered all the windows, protecting her from the sight of wrecked beaches and upended palm trees, of dying sea animals stranded on sand, dying people. She thought about her options. She did have options.

She thought about staying on the island, with José and Isabella, maybe, until she figured something out. She might work at an orphanage, caring for hurricane orphans, if there were any. She imagined waking up every morning and pouring night-chilled water into a chipped ceramic bowl, splashing awake her skin, pale under her tan. She pictured her greasy hair tied in braids under a blue and green head scarf, and the babies with their little fists in the hollows of her collarbone, gurgling along as she sang to them in English: Love is a feeling like a warm, dark stone. She would wear loose cotton blouses and long flowered skirts, work in a vegetable garden and have dirt under her fingernails like some kind of saint. She would learn Spanish, how to say, "You're welcome" without meaning "It's nothing." There were worse things a person could do with the rest of her days.

But she was already turning down the shadowy hallway that led to her room, led to her suitcase and her clothes, to the airport and her mother and her childhood bed of thick grey sheets that smelled of flowers, not of bleach or strangers' skin. Mairin remembered waking up in that bed, eight years old and afraid, the taste of rotten lemons in her throat as she called out for her mother in the darkness. She remembered opening her mouth. I threw up, Mairin had said stupidly. I'm sorry. Shh, was all her mother had said as she cuddled Mairin, the heat of her body radiating through her thin nightgown. Mairin had fallen asleep, knowing for the first time that anything could be forgiven. The bad inside of her, spilled out across the clean white carpet.

MONKFISH

EXT TO VICTOR IS AMELIA, who is worried that it still looks like she has pissed her pants. When she arrived at Kevin and Sharon's house, coincidentally at the moment that Jeremy slammed the door of their Volvo with his knee, one hand holding his tie, the other the bottles of wine, she had hopped off her bike and trotted up to him for a kiss, but he held his mouth away and looked at her crotch and said, Jesus, Amy, you look like you pissed yourself. Learn to drive, for fuck's sake.

It was almost a joke, the way he meant to say it.

There was no opportunity to fight, even though Amelia felt like beating Jeremy with her U-lock and watching him hold both hands to his nose like he was trying to push the blood back in. Kevin has a sixth sense about dinner guests, and he opened the door before they knocked. Kevin, Amelia hammed, you scared the piss out of me. Kevin hauled the bike in beside the jogging stroller. They discussed the trouble of vinyl bicycle seats while Amelia shifted back and forth in an effort to dry off. Both men smelling her.

Kevin is next to Amelia, to go along with Sharon's rules of boy girl boy girl, no spouses beside each other. Everybody but Sharon thinks that rule is pretentious, and besides, Victor messes up the system, so why bother? But Sharon is particular about her ideas. Her friends will get drunk in a respectable way and enjoy themselves at these parties. They will dress up, or at least funky. What a fun dinner party club, they'll say, toasting each other on their jobs and babies and renovated houses and funky clothes. On the eggplant and steamed pea shoots. It will make them all feel better.

Sharon, who has Jeremy on her right, has a big ass, the kind that justifies the word rump. Kevin has the idea that women should be horse-like in the way they walk: one hip bone rising as though independent of the other, proud and heavy, before dropping in a slow curve of muscle and sex. Attractive women, Kevin thinks, should make you think about childbirth, but in a sexy way. Of sex that could possibly lead to childbirth, but sex without that purpose behind it. They should smell the way Amelia smells. On his right.

Amelia's smell, more particularly Amelia, is a problem. At Amelia and Jeremy's dinner last fall, Jeremy came back from the bathroom and accidentally bumped into Kevin. Kevin, leaning against the recently refinished stairs, sloshed port on himself, staining his funky shirt. Kevin told Jeremy to watch where he was fucking going, fucking idiot. What the fuck did you say to me in my own house? Jeremy said back. Things got nasty from there.

Sharon, pregnant with Max, her swollen feet jammed into a pair of old flats, told Jeremy to back off, and Amelia (jealous of Sharon's pregnancy) told Sharon to back off herself, and the conversation of drunk or pregnant adults degenerated: Kevin telling Jeremy, You don't appreciate Amelia; Amelia telling Kevin, Kevin shut up, you're drunk, and also telling Jeremy, Kevin's drunk, don't listen to him; Sharon saying she felt crampy and wanted to go home (Max born the next afternoon, Kevin hung over); and Amelia, smoking with Victor, crying that all she wanted, fuck it, was to have a baby, but not with Jeremy, who was turning out, five years on, to be a total prick. Exhale.

Joe and Shirley were in Portugal on their belated honeymoon and missed everything.

Shirley is on the other side of Kevin, which makes Sharon feel better. Sharon doesn't appreciate Kevin and Amelia sitting beside each other, even though the whole thing, the fight, whatever it was, was almost a year ago, and everyone just wound up blaming it on the wine and then going ga-ga over Max. But still.

Sharon has the idea that Shirley tells her everything, but Shirley has not told her that Joe's doctor found a lump on his prostate. The doctor waggled his finger in my ass, Joe said. Waggle. It was ridiculous. The word kept him from crying.

Shirley is of the opinion that men don't cry unless they are dying. She saw her father cry before his quadruple by-pass surgery, and her brother, naked and bleeding from the wrists, bawled into her shoulder when she broke into his apartment and found him on the floor, fistfuls of pills scattered like confetti.

Joe (on Sharon's left) doesn't think he is dying, but he is scared of the surgery, which can cause impotence. He's heard people say that once you've been married for a while, a long while, all a person really needs is a best friend. Someone to hold hands with during movies and share the sudden orphaning that happens when parents die. Ridiculous.

Joe told Victor that making love to Shirley is the only time he's ever completely happy. They were smoking on Kevin's refinished deck. (Sharon checking on Max. Shirley stirring the sauce for her. Jeremy coming from work, Amelia on bike.) Do you know what I mean, Vic? Joe asked. Did you ever feel that way, you know, about Cathy?

Victor shook his head, and Joe resolved to sit next to him during dinner.

About Victor:

Victor's appendix burst when he was nine years old. His mother thought he was faking so he would miss a math test. He almost died.

Victor snaps a photograph of himself naked every morning. He slips it into an album. He has almost five thousand photos.

Victor's ex-wife, Cathy, is now dating a black man, and this makes Victor feel inadequate, sexually, and also racist.

No one knows any of this.

Dinner is four hours long and all they talk about is the monkfish. It is a new recipe. The monkfish is steamed and not particularly delicious, despite what everybody says.

Problem in the HAMBURGER ROOM

1. The Hamburger

THERE IS NOTHING in the first room until we get there and that is why we love it.

"This is not a gallery. It's a hallway," the guide says. We are both sympathetic towards the guide, who wears trousers one inch too short for her long and spindly legs. Such a trouser-wearer cannot be expected to know the difference between a gallery and a hallway, but having an inch less than us, as she does in several respects—not that we are bragging; we are not those kinds of men—we are inclined to think of her fondly as she studies us, the study in itself proving, among other things, that we are not in a hallway at all. We did not pay twenty dollars to see a hallway. And if we did, we will certainly demand our money back. We confer and decide to see where the gallery that may be a hallway will lead before we launch our tirade of righteous indignation upon a woman who is in need of pants with a longer inseam. We are not unnecessarily cruel. We have questions.

"No, that's an umbrella stand," the guide says.

"Yes, for umbrellas," another woman says, bobbing her head around as though she thinks this is the function of a head on a neck. Her bulgy forehead lolls towards the ground like a slave to gravity, forcing her to snap her head back every once in a while in order to keep up with the conversation. "It's just not raining today, that's probably why you were confused," she explains to us, her fat fingers dancing in a grotesque parody of raindrops, as though we did not speak the same language. Come to think of it, we do not. Come to think of it, we cannot understand a single thing she says, dancing fingers or no. She babbles on incomprehensibly and we exchange knowing glances, because we know that an astonishingly high percentage of New Yorkers are insane. Seventy-nine percent, at last count. It just happens to be the case that we are employed in the business of celebrating that fact. And we are on assignment.

"This way to the second floor," the guide says with an air of superiority.

"Baa," you and I say to each other. The insane woman overhears and raises the corners of her mouth, expressing amusement, pleasure, or approval with her face. It is amazing how barnyard animal noises can bridge barriers. Even though I am ready to crucify myself with umbrellas (there are a few) to prove my willingness to suffer for art, we follow our guide. We did not pay twenty dollars to be left behind.

But there is a problem in the hamburger room:

"I don't get it," says an old man with a cane. "What is it?"

"It's a giant hamburger," his wife says.

"I know it's a hamburger. I'm not an idiot."

"Well then, why did you ask me?" she says.

"What do you think of this?" (He is asking us, for he can sense that we are arbiters of taste.) "Is this what passes for art nowadays?"

Some questions answer themselves by being asked. We say nothing except to each other.

"Do you think they have hamburgers in the restaurant here?"

"They have a restaurant here?"

"Yes, and I could really go for a hamburger." Somebody famous said that. Not the part about the hamburgers. The part about questions answering themselves. I said it. At least I thought it. Being that it is much harder to think something than it is to say it, and also much harder to say a thing than it is to do it, I think it is fairly self-evident that I do a lot of hard work. My position as a contributing member of society cannot be disputed.

"How much do you think this'd sell for?" the old man asks with a persistence that must have been instilled in the Great Depression or the Great War, whenever it was that he ate nothing but cabbage and wore his malnourished flesh like a badge of honour.

"I think I'll have a cheeseburger," you say.

"Seriously, this is what passes for art nowadays? Giant hamburgers?" the old man says again to no one in particular.

"Actually," our guide says, "it's what passed for art in the eighties." I have a new appreciation for gallery employees the world over.

"Christ, what's the point?" the man says. He is obviously missing the apocalyptic connection between the burger and his own mortality, between art and death.

"The point of art is the end of art. Art wants to put itself out of business, out of its own misery!" I shout.

"Shh," you say.

"I think I'll have a cheeseburger too," I whisper back.

We consider another piece. It is a giant plaque. It was generously donated, a little plaque next to it tells us, by someone with a name so aristocratic I can barely make out the letters. Something like, Pierpointmorgansonrockefellersworthberg. The giant plaque, which the little plaque tells me is called "Art" and measures eighteen feet by thirty-six feet, says: Ego, by Me.

"Put that in your pipe and smoke it!" I say, not without some malice.

"Ceci n'est pas une pipe," you say. You light a cigarette for dramatic effect and we are kicked out of the gallery, without enough time to pick up our umbrellas, should we have brought them.

I am at a loss, confounded by the subjectivity of metaphor.

I renew my suggestion for cheeseburgers.

2. Dead Things in the Air and Elsewhere

"I don't understand the need for this," you say as you are searched by a fat man with some sort of beeping baton. "This is an indignity. Do you know who I am?"

The fat man does not respond, obviously embarrassed by the fact that he does not know, or possibly the man is a deaf-mute. Possibly this is why his employers have given him a beeping baton.

"Communication technologies are the hallmark of the modern age. You may quote me on that," I tell the fat, possible deaf-mute as I am asked to remove my shoes.

"For the last time, please remove your shoes, sir," a woman in a uniform says. She evidently is not a deaf-mute, just culturally undereducated. There is no excuse for this, and I blame the public school system, the clergy, the government in power, the previous generation, and the general lack of appreciation for the arts.

"This is a travesty of justice," I say.

"No, sir," she says, "this is JFK security."

I am so glad to be leaving New York, where all the escaped mental patients think they have a sense of humour.

"Destination, sir?" the woman with my shoes asks.

"Destination?" I say. "Up, most definitely. Up into the cloudless climes and starry skies, or somewhere in the general vicinity, at least."

"Business or pleasure?" she asks.

"Pleasure, always pleasure. I never conduct any business." This statement is somewhat truer than I would like. It is degrading to soar among the heavens on one's way to the glittering galas of Europe when one is lodged in economy seating next to a plaid shirt, overstuffed with skin, connected to a potato chip-smelling mouth that insists on telling all within smelling distance about the tire business in New Jersey. But our magazine is working very hard to increase its readership, and these things take time.

I explain this to the woman who has my shoes, and all she says is, "Have a nice flight." I start to suspect that everyone in New York is not crazy, but rather that everyone in New York is a robot. This is the new millennium and I am shocked by nothing, least of all by mechanical people. Mechanical people are not new, I suspect. Rather, I'm inclined to believe that the mechanizations have just made their way to the surface.

Now we can see what was always there, clanking underneath.

You are waiting at our gate, looking through a dirty window at the jet in which we will be flying. "In some cultures, to travel in the air is to go against the gods," you say.

"Really, which gods would those be?"

"Dead ones, obviously."

"Right, God is dead, in both the singular and the plural. But you have a rosary." I point to the beads twisting wildly in your hands.

"I have a fear of flying, so I prefer not to take chances."

"I have a fear of flying too." I walk you over to an airport bar, conveniently located a mere promenade from the machine that will hurtle us into the sky with all the fury of those dead animals that have become increasingly combustible over the past few million years. It is a kind of recycling program: ashes to ashes, dust to dust. This is what our dead gods intended.

"I'll have a martini," you say.

"We don't do martinis here," the bartender says with a look in his eye that seems to suggest he doesn't trust fashionably dressed men in Italian leather shoes.

"What do you do?" you ask.

"Beer," he says proudly. Apparently he invented the drink himself.

We sip our beers and for some strange reason this causes both of us to feel more connected to the earth: rotten plants and dead animals. Planes into air. Bodies into pulp. God into death. Robots with beeping batons. "The circle of life!" I say, and we drink to that. "Speed!" you say, and we drink to that. "Death!" I say, and we drink to that. "ART!" we say together, and drink to that, intoxicated by what we suspect is much more than pilsner lager. As we drink we become our own work of art, writing ourselves with every laugh and slurp, wondering how it is that so many people refuse to be their own authors.

"That's just it," you say. "There are no more people. Only robots. And robots can't write worth a damn!" You smash your glass on the floor, a gesture I respect: you always know how to round out a good idea. The bartender, however, does not appreciate the finer qualities of the English language. There is some suggestion that uniformed robots will be coming soon to deal with us, and as neither of us feels particularly interested in dealing with any more artificial life than is absolutely necessary to sustain our own, we run. This, I suggest, shows that we have a sense of humour and are therefore not robots, but rather animals. Indeed, we run with the reckless abandon of animals who one day will be dead; of animals who will use dead animals to launch themselves, dying as they are, closer to the sun, which is only partially visible from the double-paned window of a jumbo jet with exits located at the front, side, and back. Take note of the safety card in your seat pocket. In the unlikely event of a water landing, put on your lifejacket, slide down one of the rubber slides. Refrain from jumping about like animals close to death.

"I wanted the aisle seat," you say, and I come to understand sacrilege.

3. Antelopes and Other Fashionable Ladies

Someone famous is now two and a half hours late, and so consequently young people with clipboards and headsets are frantic and a woman with an unseen and exotic pet in her purse is demanding a dish and a bottle of distilled water. Of course, no one is naming names, but we anticipate a lady of a certain age and British accent who will be wearing a short skirt of the style designed to make people say, My God, I wish I had thighs like that, even though nobody has thighs like that, not even the lady in question. But still we want to see her in the hopes that a flake of her shed skin will land on us as she breezes by, and we will imagine that it is a piece of her halo breaking off. Despite the fact that there must be girls backstage taping their breasts into mesh halter tops, we feel compelled to look at the empty chair that is cordoned off with a ribbon of white silk. From our previous experiences with giant hamburgers, we know that a cordon means art. We didn't fly here defying unknown, potentially dead gods for nothing.

There are protesters outside with placards that read, Faites attention! We are not sure to what, other than the cordoned-off empty chair, but we agree, and so while waiting we join in with the chant that is slipping itself through the doors the clipboard people are opening and closing, opening and closing to the rhythm of their heartbeats: Animals are people, too! People are animals! Suddenly another, somewhat complementary chant springs up: Women are people, too! We object to objectification!

"Repetition is the sincerest form of stupidity," you say to me between chants.

We continue chanting because we are bored and because we know that eighty-three percent of Parisians are insane. It is fine to shout about wanting to be women who want to be people. We are inside the protective circle of diaphanous gowns and outrageously applied eyeshadow. Everything is simply fabulous.

"Simply fabulous," I say to the craggy-faced woman with the microphone. "I love it because it's so wearable. I think it really speaks to what women want nowadays, which is to be treated like people."

"Yes," you say, "people who are animals!" You embarrass me when you take a sly, claw-like swipe at the camera, but what does it matter. It's only television.

Then I am no longer embarrassed, or bored, or just pretending to be bored for effect, but I am happy. Happy and I know it. I clap my hands.

The black man is seven feet tall and wearing mink. His walking stick raps along the floor with a noise that sounds like take-that-and-take-that, and take it we do, for who is going to object to the sounds of a seven-foot, mink-clad black man? There is always a chance that I was wrong about the death of the divine.

Out of the penumbra of this Goliath appears a Venus, caressed by a dress the colour of lilies gone bad, and carrying a fan, perhaps to encourage enthusiasm from the nipples of the mesh-shirted models, who are only just beginning to teeter their way around. Yes, the lights are dimmed and the music thumps inside my ribcage, but I cannot turn my attention away from this lady seated eight rows ahead and to my right, behind a silk ribbon.

"It's starting," you whisper to me.

"I know," I say, looking, "but the show must go on."

Darkness overtakes the crowd, and we are forced to watch the stage. This speaks volumes about the way people think of art: they love the scenery, but can't find the subject. They aren't selling art on stage, those hawkers of mesh and tit. They just dress up women who look like antelopes and call it art, attaching a price tag for authenticity. They sell the simulacra, but they are content to let the real thing sit in the darkness with her sunglasses on, when anybody knows that she needs light to shine. I'm putting that in my review. Not the part about the reflection, but the part about the antelopes. This is why I do what I do—I see the truth in advertising. Looking at the male models, I realize they all have the sharp eyes of lynx. This can't be an accident. Not in a business where women are girls are antelopes are the antimatter between silk and chiffon.

"La femme, ce n'est jamais ça," says a woman sitting next to me. She nods as though it were a cultural activity, which it is in certain circles in Paris. To nod is not necessarily to agree, but rather to include oneself in what potentially suggests exclusion. To nod is to accept.

"Why is it the women all look like antelopes?" you ask me, and I suddenly realize why we are such a good match. Professionally. That's as far as my interest goes, the fact that I fell asleep on your shoulder during the plane ride notwithstanding, though your eyes are very blue.

"Do you think it's a birth defect," you continue, "or just some kind of eye-on-the-side-of-the-head aesthetic?"

"These girls are just too modern for their own good."

"Do they sell hamburgers here, or are the French not very into that?" you ask.

Now the chants are coursing in over the music: fur is murder, leather is death. The antelopes look skittish. The man in the mink coat is on a cellphone, escorting his Wilting Lily out a side entrance, and over a loudspeaker no one knew existed, a voice as deep and as intimidating as a god's says, "Children of the new generation, do not be afraid."

For a moment I think people are having seizures, but it turns out that they are dancing, flailing their arms and legs with deliciously reckless abandon, kicking over chairs, roaring with pleasure as they vomit champagne into their handbags, scaring the antelopes. One of the lynx pounces and brings an antelope to the floor, her tits still snug in her shirt, thanks to the technological miracle of double-sided tape. The lynx and the antelope roll about violently, until the antelope hits the lynx in the head with a folding chair with white silk ribbon on it.

"The animal kingdom," you say as we watch transfixed. There is a bartender abandoning his post. The champagne bottles sweat dejectedly and we know that some injustices cannot stand. We've a long night ahead of us, and a man cannot write without refreshment. We gather the perspiring beauties in our arms and make our way to the dance floor. We have work to do.

"Hello," I say into my phone as we dance, "Marjorie? Take this down."

We sip from the bottles and wait for the morning papers. The Word is now ours, Marjorie our secretary-Moses, and we are waiting for our disciples to flock to the magazine sellers and the street vendors. We swagger down the street. We have lost our money and our plane tickets, and forgotten where our hotel is, if we even had a hotel in the first place. But there are much more important things to worry about.

The show, you say to one scandalized old lady walking a dog, must go on.

The
D AND D REPORT

THE DEAD BOY'S NAME was Ronaldo Diaz. I remember that he drowned at a public pool in Chicago during the family swim hour. He was a weak swimmer, the newspaper said, who managed to slip into line for the waterslide and get lost in the splash of other, happy children. He was an only child, and he was there alone. His mother, a single parent who worked the day shift at Safeway and the night shift at Fresh 'n' Go Variety, had sent him to the pool because it was only June and already a vicious summer, the kind that made the city open emergency cooling centres for homeless people and initiate rolling brownouts. Mrs. Diaz was quoted as saying that all she wanted was for Ronnie to have a little fun after school. She didn't have air conditioning and the pool was free—what else was she supposed to do? "All those lifeguards are white," Mrs. Diaz told the reporter. "You tell me why they didn't see him." There was going to be an inquest.

The picture of Ronnie was a school photo. He had on a dress shirt, which was carefully ironed and buttoned to his neck. Over the shirt he wore a chain, and at the end of it was a small cross. At least I thought it was a cross, but it was hard to tell from the grainy photo. There was something around the boy's neck, that was for sure, and the neck itself made me think the kid would have grown up to be a bruiser, a guy with a shaved head and big muscles, a girlfriend he watched like a jealous dog. He was just a kid—only nine, the head-line said—but he had the look. Thick dark hair and a strong chin he pushed out, daring the photographer to take the picture as he bared his teeth. His mother probably loved his fat cheeks, but that kind of softness sent boys to the gym to toughen up once they made it to high school. It gave them something to prove.

I slid the photocopy over to Cheryl's half of the desk. Len was at the front of the staff room, jabbing the paper with his index finger the way a pigeon pecks a stale piece of bread.

"This," he said, his sandals squeaking as he paced in front of the blackboard, "this is what I'm talking about when I talk about a lack of communication. How did this kid get any-where near the slide without doing a deep end test? There but for the grace of G-O-D, people." He spelled out the let-ters, sticking his paper to the board with a magnet that said Stay Alert, Stay Safe 1999. Cheryl kicked me under the desk, then made fists, closing her eyes and rubbing her knuckles together before jolting herself awake with mimed defibrilla-tor paddles. "Today," Len went on, "the D and D Report is about waterslide safety." He tightened his ponytail, which was tinged slightly green from chlorine, and looked us over like a gung-ho missionary. Cheryl rolled her eyes. Our pool didn't have a waterslide.

Most of the other lifeguards, even the few who were actual adults with children and cars, thought that Len was a weirdo and a pervert, a grown man who lived with his mother and made a habit of picking the girls with the biggest breasts for the CPR booster sessions. I thought him strange too, the way his skin repelled water like a rubber tarp and left him bone dry on the deck while the rest of us stood hunched and goosebumped, shivering until training was over. The sleekness of his ponytail was the only sign that Len had ever been in the water. "It looks like a leaky ferret, or something," Cheryl had said on my first day. "It's like, 'Dude, the 1980s called, and they want their deadbeat dad hair back.'" Then she had asked me if it was true that I was in university, and could I buy her a mickey of vodka for Friday night. After that, we were friends.

It was Cheryl who came up with the name for the weekly briefing: the Dead and Deader Report. All of us, even Len, to his credit, called it the D and D. The D and D consisted of Len bringing in articles about people dying, or almost dying, in swimming pools, usually after doing something stupid. There was the guy who took a swan dive off a hotel balcony into a wading pool during frosh week, and the parents who let their five-year-old cook her brain in a hot tub while they went to the swim-up bar. Each week, Len passed out a new article, and we were supposed to talk about how we, as responsible lifeguards, would have prevented the incident. His point was simple. "The problem is that most people think we save lives," he said. "The fact is, if you have to save somebody, you've already screwed up." Cheryl agreed Len had a point there, but that was mostly because she flirted her way through her exams and didn't know a Pia

Carry from a Heimlich manoeuvre. She usually tried to take shifts with one of the adult lifeguards, in particular a woman with flabby thighs we called the Diving Board Nazi. "She scares people out of the pool," Cheryl said with admiration. "It's awesome."

Once Cheryl told me that the D and D had been a story from our own pool. "A woman miscarried in the ladies' locker room at the end of Aquafit," she said. "The thing looked like a wet kitten. I swear to God, it was covered in fur."

"You're disgusting."

"I swear to God," she said again. "I found her. It was really freaky. The Nazi took a whole month off after, and I still won't go in that shower without wearing flip-flops."

It might have been true. Since then, I have seen enough bodies in various stages of birth and death to know that almost anything is possible, but back then my medical knowledge came primarily from biology textbooks and re-runs of *ER*. I was skeptical, and Cheryl was always making up stories.

I thought that there were only two kinds of people, generally speaking: the kind that got more embarrassed when they put on a bathing suit, and the kind that got less. The confident ones—fitness buffs in neon bathing caps, elderly women with elephantine breasts—came for the lap swim, and they knew their limits. Most of the time it was safe for me to zone out to the sounds of people sluicing down the lanes. Sometimes I got so relaxed I felt like my eyes detached from my brain and floated on the surface of the pool, buoyed along in the wake of perfectly automated flutter kicks. It was like watching incredibly boring trained seals. At least the cocky ones gave me something to watch. Spindly girls in biki-nis begged for attention as they shrieked and grabbed each

other by the elbows, sliding around on the wet pool deck
in the hopes that a boy might find the nerve to push them
in. The worst I expected there was a bloody nose, maybe a
chipped tooth. I only had to blow my whistle a few times before one of them inevitably called me a bitch, or something
similar, and then the gaggle of them would decide to leave.

It was the shy ones I worried about the most. They were
the ones who had heart attacks in locked bathroom stalls,
seizures behind shower curtains. Kids who were afraid to tell
their parents they had choked back pool water ended up
dying later of secondary drowning, their lungs filling with
suffocating white froth as they slept. When these people got
into trouble, and especially if they thought they were dying,
they wanted to be left alone. They hid. They were like animals that way.

It strikes me now that Ronnie Diaz didn't fit into either
category. He may have had the guts to try the waterslide,
but by all accounts he never called for help, or even splashed
around. He simply jumped in and disappeared, sinking to
the bottom like a perfectly weighted anchor.

But I didn't think about that at the time. I was bored and
hot in the stuffy room, and Ronnie Diaz was just another
D and D Report. I remember Len finished diagramming a
search pattern on the blackboard—"We'll call this the Diaz
Pattern," he said, and Cheryl made a small horking noise—
and then the staff meeting was over. Len exhaled like a
deflating balloon as we handed him back our photocopies,
or threw them in the garbage.

"We going to your house?" Cheryl said, which was her
way of saying that we were.

The parking lot asphalt radiated the heat of the day
back at us, sucking at the cheap rubber of my sandals as we

walked to the bus stop. We sat in the bus shelter, ignoring the fact that it was essentially a greenhouse.

"The problem with this job," Cheryl said, digging through her purse, "is that the human body is disgusting and dangerous. When you dress it in Lycra and put it in water, it only gets worse." She found a lollipop and unwrapped it with her teeth, spitting the wrapper onto the ground. "What other job issues you a special net for skimming poop? There was a kid the other day who barfed and shat in the pool at the same time. Come *on*."

The foulings, as Len called them, were secretly my favourite part of the job—if it was bad enough, I got to close out the pool and get paid to sit in the staff room and do nothing, or my homework. I was working on applications for medical school, and I was finding the essays difficult: why did I want to be a doctor, and what did compassionate care mean to me? I spent a lot of time on my laptop, Googling the answers to these personal questions and checking my email.

Cheryl licked her arm and smelled the skin. "What does this smell like to you, Alexa?"

"I'm not smelling your arm."

"Chlorine," she said definitively. "Len shocks the hell out of that pool. I've had to buy two bathing suits this year alone. It's a miracle we have any skin left."

Cheryl and I heard the rattle of the city bus and she tucked the lollipop into her cheek. We grabbed our bags and stood outside the shelter, the whine of the bus engine making us wrinkle our noses in anticipation of the hot soot. The driver saw us, waved, and flicked his sign over to "Not in Service." The bus kicked up a hot wind as it whooshed past us,

and we went back into the greenhouse without saying anything. We didn't take it personally.

After a while, Cheryl asked, "You're pre-med, right? What
does that even mean, pre-med?"

"It means," I said, holding my hands out so as to read
from an invisible piece of paper, "that Alexandra Turner's
work as a lifeguard shows her commitment to saving lives."

The silence of the bus shelter sounded like a shell pressed
to my ear, hollow and roaring at the same time. I dropped
my hands into my lap.

"You save lives." Cheryl sucked on her lollipop. "Well,
I'm impressed. Give this girl a medal."

"I'm still working on the application," I said. "Forget
about it."

I was relieved to hear the drone of a new bus and I stood
up before realizing it was only the welling buzz of cicadas.
I sat back down on the bench, hugging my backpack, and I
licked my arm. "It does smell like chlorine," I said. I wanted
to change the subject.

Cheryl took the lollipop out of her mouth and tossed it
on the ground. She rolled it back and forth under her foot
like she was working an old-fashioned sewing machine.
"You're never going to get in with that kind of stuff," she
said. "Saving lives? You might as well say you're in it for the
money. At least that'd be more original."

I knew she was right. All the application guides I read
said my personal essay should be about something riveting
and emotional, or at least violent. Good topics included my
own past experience with a doctor—bonus points if I had
suffered from a serious or chronic illness—or a relative
dying in a long, drawn-out way. The samples on the internet

were full of that kind of stuff: a guy who helped his mother shave her head before chemo; a rape crisis counsellor who convinced a suicidal woman to go to the emergency room. My favourite essay was about an AIDS hospice worker who had been born in what he called "abject Beirut," losing both his parents in a bus bombing before moving to America to heal people. I was white and from the suburbs; my grandmother paid my college tuition and all my other expenses. I lived twenty minutes away from my mom and dad, and I had never seen a dead body.

"Don't worry," Cheryl said. "I got you covered." She looked up and down the street and then tied her hair back with a rubber band. "Check this out. You know that woman in the shower, the one who had the miscarriage?"

I felt the air in my lungs compress a little like I was diving under water, a feeling made more real by the sight of a bus shimmering towards us in the heat. "Let's go," I said, standing. "He's not going to see us in here."

"It was the Diving Board Nazi who actually found her," Cheryl went on. "She called me in and told me to put on a pair of gloves and pick up the baby—she called it a baby. She said to wrap it in a towel and give it to the mother. The thing was a mutant, Alex. It looked like E.T. for God's sake. It was obviously dead, but the Nazi was like, 'Be careful to support her head.'"

"Jesus. Let's go." The bus was almost there, and I didn't like where Cheryl was going. I was out of breath in the thick, wet heat. The smell of chlorine—it was not just on my skin, I realized, but in my hair and on my clothes—was making me feel sick.

"Her head," Cheryl said again, not moving. "That woman was just leaning against the wall, her skin almost the same colour as the white tile, and there was blood everywhere. The Diving Board Nazi was doing something, I don't know what, between her legs, but this woman didn't take her eyes off me as I bundled her baby. She had these really dark eyes, almost black, or I thought she did. It turned out that they were just all pupil."

"What is wrong with you?" I shouted as the bus pulled up and opened its doors. I jumped onto the first step. "Cheryl!"

"Relax, Alex." Cheryl stood up and cocked her hip, giving me the same face she gave Len when he told her that lifeguards were required to wear regulation sweatpants. She jammed her hand into her pocket, calmly searching for a ticket as the bus driver tried to shut the doors on me. "Is this or is this not the kind of shit that gets you in?" she said.

I admitted that it was.

Cheryl pushed past me to pay her fare and then strolled to the back of the empty bus, swinging herself along the fabric loops that dangled from the ceiling, her feet just barely touching the floor like she was floating through space.

"We're writing your essay tonight," she said.

We took the bus to my apartment. We sat on my bed and I gave Cheryl my laptop, but before we started I told her I had thought about it, and I didn't want to use the baby story after all. I wanted my essay to be about Ronnie Diaz.

"What? Why?" Cheryl squinted at me like I was out of focus, or crazy. "The baby thing is way better."

"It just feels too, I don't know, too personal, or something. Like I'm taking advantage."

"Personal is good," Cheryl said. "And you are taking advantage. That's the point. Come on, I'll even leave out the part about the fur."

I refused. I didn't believe the story, not entirely, but I still couldn't bring myself to trade on a dead baby in a shower stall. It seemed like the kind of thing I might regret, years later. I believed in karma then. I wanted to have children some day.

Cheryl tried to point out the fact that I'd be denying myself the opportunity to save hundreds of babies. "If you tell them you want to be an obstetrician," she said, "this thing'll write itself."

In the end she wrote the essay about Ronnie Diaz—"It's your funeral," she shrugged—changing names and geographies, adding details about my dramatic and ultimately unsuccessful attempts at CPR. We both agreed that tragedy, not heroism, was the better strategy. She called the essay, "Why I Want to Be a Doctor"; she said that a more inventive title wasn't necessary. "You need to blend in just enough," she advised. "They have to go in expecting crap and come out bawling."

I promised to mail it in the next day, and to tell Cheryl as soon as I heard anything.

Not long after, though, I got a job as a research assistant in the biology lab. It paid better than the pool, and I thought it looked good on my resume. I quit lifeguarding, and I lost track of Cheryl.

I didn't think of her again until the acceptance letters came. I had aced my school interviews by repeating the Ronnie Diaz story, almost exactly as she had written it. I opened each crisp, thick envelope with a kind of sensual pleasure, leafing through the glossy brochures of smiling but serious people in preppy blazers and polo shirts. One of the pamphlets said that sixty-five percent of doctors meet their future partners at medical school. I was ecstatic. I called my parents

to give them the news, and they asked me to make a reserva-
tion at the fanciest restaurant in town. We were celebrating
my bright future. They said I should bring a friend, but by
then Cheryl didn't work at the pool anymore. I heard from
Len that she had quit to audition for an arts school in the
city. Acting, he said, or writing. He wasn't sure. "She gave me
one day's notice," he said, "and now I'm scrambling to staff
Family Swim."

I told myself it was probably too late to find her.

I MET DARREN during a cardiology rotation. When we married, the tables at our reception were named for parts of
the heart: we sat the wedding party at Aorta, our parents at
Superior Vena Cava, that kind of thing. The flowers for the
tables were arranged in beakers and flasks, and we served
gazpacho appetizers in test tubes. We designed a monogram
of hummingbirds in a stylized heart, the twigs in their beaks
intertwining in a double helix to spell DnA for our initials.
We printed it on programs that doubled as fans—it was
August, and we had rented a tent for my grandmother's garden. After the ceremony, people toasted us with champagne,
and then servers in impossibly crisp white shirts brought
around drinks that looked like parrots, bright red with lime
wedge tails. My father told them to keep them coming all
night. My mother had found an antique bird cage and spray-
painted it gold, setting it on the gift table as a moneybox
with a sign that read, Help the Lovebirds Feather Their Nest.
Darren told her he thought it was unnecessary; didn't we
already have everything we had ever wanted? My mother was
charmed all over again.

After I cut the cake and tossed the bouquet, I slipped
away to the front of the house. I took off my shoes and lay

down on the prickly grass, spreading my arms wide as I looked up into the milky grey sky. The jazz band was playing a slow number, and the music mixed with the pieces of conversation that floated across the lawn like friendly ghosts. I closed my eyes until all I heard was the thrumming of the party, like a pulse, and I thought, happily, This is what it must feel like to be dead. No, not dead, I corrected myself. Unborn. Brand new.

"What's up, Doc?"

I sat up and opened my eyes and there she was. Her hair was cut unfashionably short and pinned behind each ear with drugstore barrettes. With one hand she balanced a tray of parrot cocktails, a thick napkin over her forearm, and with the other she untucked her white shirt, which was too big for her in the body, boxy like it belonged to a man. It made her look thin in an unsettling way; she reminded me of a patient in a hospital gown. She set the tray between us and put the napkin over her shoulder, as though she were getting ready to burp a baby. She picked a lime wedge from one of the glasses, sucking on it a bit before chucking it into the bushes and sitting down beside me, scratching at her back. "They bleach the shit out of these things. It gives me a rash."

"Cheryl. What are you doing here?" My voice was sticky, as though I'd been asleep.

"This was supposed to be my weekend off, but I switched when I saw the name. I was curious." Cheryl drank half her cocktail in one mouthful and crunched an ice cube. She stared at me. "That dress looks nice on you."

"My grandmother picked it." I flounced the skirt, keeping my eyes on the ground.

"And he seems nice. Derek."

"Darren," I said, picking at the grass. "I heard you were going to arts school."

Cheryl finished her drink and started in on another. "Len's dying."

"What?"

"Something eating his lungs into Swiss cheese, and he's suing the pool."

"Jesus."

She shrugged. "It's probably his own fault. I smelled like chlorine for years after I left. That kind of thing catches up to you, eventually."

We sat on the lawn and stared out into the street, sipping our drinks and watching cars drive by. A few of them honked when they saw me in my wedding dress and veil, and I raised my glass in a salute to their enthusiasm about my new life. I turned to salute Cheryl too, hoping to look open-hearted and forthcoming, newly cleansed by a ritual that had required me to wear white and carry flowers, to be led down a walkway by small children throwing rose petals. But Cheryl was already finished her drink and starting to tuck in her shirt. "If my boss sees me, I'll get fired. No drinking on the job, no mixing with the clients."

"But we're friends," I said.

Cheryl stopped and squinted at me, one hand down the back of her pants. Her mouth opened and it was a good two seconds before any sound came out. "Don't," she said flatly, like she had considered her options and it was the only word worth the effort.

She stood and balanced her empty glass on one side of the tray, repositioning the napkin over her arm. She straightened her spine and gave her head a little shake to the left, the same way she used to when there was water in her ear.

I wanted to say something redemptive and apologetic, or at least something that might ring even partly true, but instead I asked her about Ronaldo Diaz.

"Do you ever think about that kid?" I said.

"What kid?"

"From the essay. Ronnie Diaz."

Cheryl laughed and the crack of it startled me. "Ronnie Diaz was a piece of newsprint, Alex."

I watched her walk back towards the house. My eyes strained as parts of her vanished: first her black pants, then her outstretched arm, then even the electric whiteness of her shirt melted into the shadows. I was struck by the fact that, at a certain distance, everything blends into the background.

Later that night I found out that the bird cage full of envelopes was missing. "Stolen," my grandmother declared. She called it a violation. She wanted to call the police, interrogate the catering staff—"They were the only ones with access," she said, "the only ones who weren't family or friends." I told her I would handle it. It was probably all just a misunderstanding, I said. Nothing just disappears.

The METEORITE HUNTER

DAVID'S FIRST THOUGHT when she was born was that she was dead. She was blue and rubbery, rimed in thick whiteness like a freezer-burned steak. All lumps of fat flesh and shivery lengths of bone, fists clenched and ready to fight their way into an afterlife that had already started there on the starched sheet, stained with tired blood and greasy lubricant. Her name was going to be Lily, because it had sounded sweet and pure and clean and white. But that was before they saw her there, dead and turning purple.

"Oh fuck," Julie said, and those were the first words the dead baby heard, her heart still beating, her mouth open.

David almost had the courage to reach between his baby's blackened lips with a hooked finger. Something he had seen on television somewhere. Something a father would do. But the doctor, wearing a bandana patterned with cowboys roping steer, swooped in and picked her up, twisting her upside down and holding onto her neck while her body sat limp on his forearm, barely making it to his elbow. He slapped his gloved fingers against her blue backside.

"Come on, girl," he said, slapping her again before flipping her over his arm and sucking the snot and phlegm out of her nose and mouth with what looked to David like an enema bulb. "That's right, come on," the doctor said, slapping.

She didn't come on. They took her to a table under a bright light and spoke incantations of acronyms, taping electrodes to her ribs and shoving a long and silvery plastic tube down her nose and into her flat belly. David looked on while Julie, numb from the waist down, legs flopping out of the stirrups, yelled at the nurses, "Is she okay? Is she okay?"

No, their aproned backs said. She is not okay.

Another doctor came to work on Julie with thick and steady hands that scared David. "It's alright, sir," the doctor had said. "You can go with your daughter."

David wondered if everyone saw right through him.

Once his baby stopped dying and started breathing, he held her in his arms and thought about what kind of warrior name he should give the baby girl who used to be called Lily. A name that had some strength to it, some meat. A name that would ward off the curses of birth trauma. Muscle weakness. Brain damage.

"David." Julie's voice was soft as she reached for the baby with her long, white arms.

"Let's name her Diana," David said.

Julie looked at the baby and at David in his running shoes and faded t-shirt, his beard red and grey, his hands clumsy as he passed his daughter to her mother.

"I love you, Deedee. You did good," Julie had said to the baby who came back from the dead, as if it were the easiest thing in the world.

And it had been easy then, David thought, looking over at the awkward contortion of girl that Diana was now, all elbows and knees beside him in the front seat of the rusted-out Rabbit. Her face was pressed against the passenger side window as she slept. He thought about reaching over and brushing the hair from her forehead, but he didn't want her to wake up and look him in the eye. It was better just to drive.

He wanted to pull over soon, even if it was a long way to Whiteshell and Rick had told him to get there fast.

"We don't want *Explore* to hear about this guy, Dave," he had said. "There just aren't enough crazy Indian stories to go around these days."

Rick in David's cubicle, wearing those hiking boots that squeaked on the office carpet, which was made of reconstituted pop bottles, didn't David know. Rick's khakis pouching around his crotch as he sat on the edge of David's desk.

"The guy is an obvious nut job, but whatever, right? People are into that kind of New Age bullshit. Makes our readers feel more connected to the land, whatever, whatever. Call him The Meteorite Hunter, or something. Yeah. Write that down."

David wrote it down.

"Make sure you get a shot of him all mystical. Looking up at the sky, holding the meteorites like he's talking to the bloody aliens."

"Aliens, right."

"But don't get too bogged down in the science," Rick said. "All people need to know is that shit falls from space and then this guy finds it and picks it up. But stress the Native thing. Seriously, it's nothing without the Indian connection. Hell, the world could probably learn a thing or two from wackos like this. And it's a long drive to Whiteshell."

"Already said."

Rick had walked away from the desk in his wool socks and leather boots like he was climbing Mount Kilimanjaro. Well, David had been camping, too. Once. Julie's idea. He still remembered the image of her legs planted in an upside down V as she waited under the canoe for him to catch up on the portage. David, puffing and pale. His skin clammy and his ass itchy. Nothing left to do but hump the pack while Julie called out, You okay? Fine, David thought, heart exploding. Yes. The smell of Julie on his body mixing with his sweat, the smoke in his hair, the grit in his teeth.

Julie. Her voice into his blood like a heart attack when she called:

"David? It's me."

His fingers had gone numb at the sound of her taking in a breath. By the way she said his name.

"David, are you there?"

She had told him she was sorry that everything was last minute, that he hadn't seen Diana for so long. No, she was sure she didn't want Deedee at the funeral, she needed to go alone. It was okay with her if Diana went to Whiteshell, as long as he swore up and down that the car was in okay shape and he could have Diana back on the bus by Sunday afternoon.

"David, can you handle this?"

David had hung up the phone and looked again at the map, retracing his route along the Trans-Canada highway with a dull pencil. Nothing left to do but drive.

And now Diana was snoring, thick little gasps that made David nervous. He went faster still, racing the sun to the horizon.

*   *   *

"Do you have to go to the bathroom?" David asked.

"No," Diana said, rubbing her eyes.

"Are you sure? 'Cause we can't stop for a while, and . . ." David trailed off, wondering if ten-year-olds still pissed themselves every once in a while. He had no idea.

"I know. I'm fine." Her voice like Julie's. All sass and pity.

"Are you hungry?" he asked. "Do you like hamburgers?"

"I'm not really supposed to eat them. Mom says that they feed the cows unhealthy things, like antibiotics and ground-up animals. Makes you sick."

"Yeah," David said, eyes on the road, watching for deer. "I guess that probably isn't too good." Shit, Julie.

She yawned. "But what doesn't kill you makes you stronger, right?"

"Where'd you get that?"

Diana shrugged. "Oprah."

David glanced over as she talked, watching her so-what palms punctuate her sentences. You still drive the Rabbit, she had said as they walked across the empty bus station parking lot, careful not to make it a question. That's cool, she added. Sensitive, for a ten-year-old. Brave to travel alone, to carry her backpack so casually over just one shoulder. Now her fingers, pink and raw like skinny newborn mice, were finding the holes in the upholstery, burrowing. One day she would be pretty, David hoped.

She hugged her knees as she talked, her feet weaving back and forth across the dashboard leaving behind a figure-eight of dust from the dried mud on her sneakers. Her grey eyes reflected the high beams of passing cars, like she was lit up from the inside. Then a blurry little halo of hands because she was excited. That. That he knew. That was all Julie.

"But what do you think?" she asked, eyes on him. High beams.

Shit.

"Are you listening to me?"

"I'm listening," David said, eyes on the road. "It's just hard to know what to think sometimes."

"Yeah, but if Mom had her way, we'd all be living in teepees and eating organic rocks, or whatever." Diana looked out the window. "How much longer?"

"Maybe we'd be better off," David said. He pushed harder on the accelerator.

It was all Julie's fault, in a way. She had landed him the job at the magazine. Begged it for him. Five months pregnant then and constipated. Her hands like rabid bats, flying into her hair as she said to David, Well, what the hell do you think it's going to eat? Breast milk until it goes to college? David worked at the grocery store, knew the codes for all the produce: 4020, Golden Delicious apples; 6113, kiwi fruit. He bought a crib with loose rails from a garage sale and Julie painted it yellow wearing her nurse's mask, worried about paint fumes and deformities. They fought until Julie threw a mug of green tea through the front window, but no, David still wasn't taking the job from Rick. He had cleaned up the broken glass and duct-taped a garbage bag into the frame.

There was just no way. It was a pity job, and it was from Rick. Rick the Dick. The guy who got drunk at the hospital Christmas party and grabbed Julie's ass as he said with a slurred tongue, A nurse is a wonderful thing for a woman to be. Rick's wife Tricia cried into her plastic cup of wine, her mascara plopping onto her red velvet dress. David had noticed how pretty she was, how beautiful a woman she could be with her hair in curls and her make-up running. How lovely it was when she put her soft, cool hand on his and said, Oh, David. Julie had come up to them then with their jackets in her arms, telling Tricia it was okay, they were going to have a good laugh about it all on Monday.

"For Christ's sake, let's get them home," Julie had whispered to David. He had helped Tricia button her coat.

"Sorry," he said when he touched her breasts.

David drove. Rick in the front seat, his forehead pressed against the window, unrolled a little to let in flakes of sobering snow. Julie and Tricia were in the backseat, Tricia still snuffling, but laughing here and there at Julie's little jokes. David had watched in the rear-view mirror as Tricia touched at her mascara with a tissue.

"Dad?" Diana said. "I am hungry, actually."

She pointed to a sign at the side of the road: Tasty and Delicious Diner, 1 km. A picture of a hamburger, fries. A milkshake. David checked the map again. He wasn't any closer.

*   *   *

THE HAMBURGERS were flat and steaming, served by a woman with large breasts that sagged inside her waitress blouse. Regina, her nametag read. "Enjoy your meal," she said when she plopped the plates down on the Formica table, making the pickle slices bounce. "I hope it's tasty and delicious."

Diana sat opposite him in the booth, cross-legged. She wrapped her long hair into curls around her index finger. Her eyes were puffy. She poked at the burger with her fork, sipped her chocolate milkshake. She tested a french fry and looked right at him. High beams.

"Why didn't Mom let me go with her? I'm not a little kid anymore."

"Well, she thinks you're old enough to handle a weekend with me," David said, not sure if he was joking.

Diana shrugged. "Everybody else was busy. Mom called like twenty people."

"Twenty?"

"But it wasn't like she thought it was a bad idea, or anything," Diana said quickly. "In the end, I mean." She paused.

"Listen," David said, leaning into the table, "I'm sure your mom has her reasons for why she didn't want you to go. She probably just didn't want you to have to see all that funeral stuff. It can be kind of scary." He ate his fries.

"I heard Mom say on the phone that Grandpa was a class-A shithead."

Regina came over and poured more coffee into David's cup, spilling some on the table, wiping it up with a dirty rag she took out of her apron pocket. David took out the map to Whiteshell to have something to look at.

"So, was he?" Diana, relentless.

"What?"

"A shithead."

"Diana, language." More fries in his mouth. "But yeah, sometimes. Not always, though. I don't know. It's complicated."

The last time David had pulled into the driveway of the cigarette-stained bungalow, he had heard the tinny sound of a shoot-em-up blasting out of the television and seen the stacks of stale dishes festering on the counters. There was a vase of tulips on the kitchen table, Grace's favourite, just starting to wilt.

"Hello, sir," David had said. "Julie sent me to pick up a few things for her mother. That she needs. The hospital made me a list."

"You still working at the goddamn grocery store?" The voice soggy like wet cardboard.

"Actually, I write for a magazine now. It's called *The Adventurist* and it's for men who—"

"Fucking great," Frank said, his eyes on the television. "Now get outta my house."

"I've got the list right here," David said, offering the crumpled paper and wishing he had just gone to a drugstore instead of dealing with the old prick again, regardless of what Julie said about Grace needing her own things, that patients always did better with a few things from home.

"What part of get the fuck outta here didn't you understand?"

Frank stood, his knees cracking under the weight. His flesh flowed down his body, settling somewhere in his lower gut. His face was loose and jowly, ready to stretch into tissue-thin skin. He wore an unbuttoned flannel shirt, stained jogging pants that sagged. Shoes with bursting seams like split sausages. His thick hair was perfectly combed.

"The nurses said she needs a nightgown, a toothbrush."

"Get outta my house."

Frank shuffled past David into the kitchen, his fat hands inching him along the greasy wall, the stink of liquor and sweat drifting back.

"You can just tell me where to look and I'll get them myself."

"If you don't leave, I'll make you," Frank said, his lungs whistling.

"Oh Jesus, Frank," David said. "This is ridiculous. Just give me her fucking toothbrush and I'll tell her you send your love, okay?"

Frank took the vase of tulips to the sink, filling it to the brim with cloudy water.

"Gracie is dying," Frank said, his eyes the pale blue of soft ice. "Don't you tell me about love."

David had given up and bought Grace a flannel nightgown from The Bay. Slippers. A new toothbrush, a hairbrush, and a gossip magazine. But by the time he got to the hospital, her room had been cleaned, the bed made. Julie sat on a plastic chair in the corner of the waiting room, feeding Diana and crying, her left breast leaking through her shirt.

"I'm so sorry, Julie." He let the bag of useless items drop onto the seat beside her.

"It's not his fault, Dave," she had said, wiping the tears off her lips. "I know you think it is, but it's not."

She told him that once, for her birthday, Frank had given her a beautiful doll wrapped in pink tissue paper and a white box.

"It had real glass eyes. Bright robin's egg blue." She shook her head. "The memory alone."

Julie had put Diana over her shoulder to burp her, and the sound of her hand on their baby's back had seemed shockingly hollow to David.

"Mom's just so unfair," Diana whined, her high-pitched voice carrying through the diner and making Regina raise her eyebrows.

"Finish your fries," David said, laying bills on the table. "We're leaving."

*   *   *

DAVID SAW THE HOUSE just as his eyes started to swerve
blankly across the dirt road, the sun coming up.

The small, squat cabin was built of thick timber that was
greyed with weather. Stray red and yellow leaves skittered
down the steep roof, crackling like old, dry bones. David was
going to get a picture when the sun was higher and the leaves
were spinning. When The Meteorite Hunter was backlit and
holding a blood-red stone from outer space. The kind of
picture Rick liked. He would say, Yeah, Dave, now that looks
authentic.

Diana stretched in the front seat. "I have to go to the
bathroom."

"Just go in the bushes."

"What, the Lord of the Meteorites doesn't have a bathroom?"

"Just pee in the bushes."

"This trip sucks."

"Pretend it's an adventure."

Diana slammed the car door and tramped off into the
brush, hiking up her jeans with defiant fists. David leaned
back in his seat and closed his eyes, thinking to himself what
Julie was going to say about all of this, how she might not
say anything at all, just turn away and hunch her shoulders,
curving her spine into a question mark.

It had all been so stupid. Julie knew he wasn't working on
a last-minute story for the winter issue. She had phoned the
office—four messages when he went in the next morning—
before getting him on his cell, her voice as thin as a splinter.

"Deedee's crying and the car isn't starting," she had said,
"but I need to go for a drive to calm her down. When are

you going to be home? Don't we have a computer at home? Why did we buy that fucking computer anyway?"

But David wasn't listening. He was looking at Tricia on the bed as she pulled the sheets over her breasts and brushed the bangs out of her eyes. He considered the possibility then that it had all been a weird coincidence, a trick of physics that made their respective trajectories collide, bodies tangling in the same space and the same time. It didn't mean anything. It was just the kind of accidental intimacy that comes at the end of a tense conversation, or after a long wait. Tricia said the problem was they were bored with their lives but resigned to them. They should just give up. "But I can't," David said. "That's what kills me." Once for fun they took pills that Tricia stole from the hospital and David had had an allergic reaction, his tongue swelling, his breathing panicked.

"You're the one in a million, David. Lucky you," Tricia had said then, jamming the needle of epinephrine into his thigh as she drove him to the emergency room.

"David?" Julie's voice from the phone, Tricia reaching for her robe.

"Julie," David said, "I love you, you know."

Tricia rolled her eyes and cinched the belt.

"Dave," Julie, surprised. "That's worse."

"I'll fix the Rabbit, first thing tomorrow," he said, but Julie had already hung up the phone. Tricia looked at him like she was trying to keep back a laugh.

"No offense, David," she had said, "but who drives a Rabbit?"

This trip to Whiteshell was going to wreck the car, if it hadn't already. David envisioned himself at the side of the road, working uselessly under the smoking hood, telling

Diana to stop thumbing for rides. Julie was going to be mad
if he didn't have her back for school on Monday, even if he
tried to convince her that this meteorite guy was educational
or spiritual, or even just plain crazy and interesting. David
sat up in his seat and turned the key in the ignition, to be
safe. The engine revved and Diana came running back, her
hair long and tangled, weeds catching her feet.

"Hey, kiddo," he said, leaning over to open her door, "did
you think I was leaving without you?"

Diana slammed the door behind her and locked it. She
looked at David with drowning eyes, wild and dark.

"What's wrong, Dee? Are you sick?" That hamburger.
Shit. Julie was going to kill him.

"I was just going to see if I could use the bathroom,"
Diana said, starting to cry, "I opened the door, and, that, that
man..."

David's heart cramped in his chest. She had only been
gone a minute.

"Diana, what happened?"

Fuck, that's what parents said when their children were
molested or kidnapped. A minute was more than enough.

"Diana!"

But she was sobbing so hard now she couldn't speak, her
fists balled into her eyes as her small body shook, curled up
in the front seat of the car, the mud on her shoes grinding
itself into the torn upholstery of the seat.

David ran towards the cabin. How could he have let her
go by herself? They were out in the middle of nowhere, and
this guy was some kind of crazy hermit who probably hadn't
seen anything female in years, probably had fucking booby
traps on the door and hunting knives lining the walls. Was
Diana hurt? Christ! He hadn't even checked. God.

David sprinted, bursting through the door of the cabin ready to kill the sonofabitch.

But he was already dead. The Meteorite Hunter was sitting in a chair, his face on the oily wood table, his bloated black cheek touching the rough edge of a blood-coloured rock. David might have thought he was sleeping if not for the strange and broken angle of his neck, the way his arms dangled ridiculously, his blue skin dotted with industrious ants that pooled in the rotting practice cuts on his arms, his stomach. The knife handle that stuck out of his bare chest like an accidental bone. The dried blood and the flies. The stink, like cabbage left in the sun.

"Don't come in here, Diana!" David shouted over his shoulder, knowing that it didn't matter anymore. She was sobbing in the car while David, gagging now, rushed into the stale emergency of the rank cabin, shouting brave-sounding, stupid things like Don't come in here, Diana. Shit.

David saw a pad of paper under the blood-red stone. Careful not to touch the man, David moved the rock, heavy for its size, and picked up the smudged notebook. FOUND, it said at the top. In the left-hand column was a list of numbers, latitude and longitude. Then a weather report, followed by a catalogue of stones. A record of a lifetime spent searching. David looked at Diana in the car, how small she was against the landscape of dying trees. He wondered how he was supposed to know what to find. Where to look.

The Meteorite Hunter didn't have a phone, which was no surprise. They were going to have to drive to a police station and file a report. The officers were going to ask Diana about what she saw, and what could she say to that? David looked at the Meteorite Hunter rotting in his chair. Who was going to bury him? He hoped someone was going to mourn what had been lost. That there had been something to lose, after all.

David walked slowly back to the car with the notebook in his hand, opening the passenger door as gently as he could but Diana still jumped. He picked her up and slid into the seat, rocking her as she cried.

"It's going to be okay," he said, even though he had seen the expression on the man's face, flies feasting on his eyes as they stared unblinking at the one dusty window of the cabin, the glass as thin as paper at the top of the pane. The hunter's lips were purple and peeled back from his teeth. It might have been a smile or a scream, David didn't know, but it was a silent answer to the one question he couldn't bring himself to ask.

"It's okay," David said again, and Diana buried her face in his shoulder the way she had done as a baby, tired and squalling. It was almost a selfish thought, but he knew there was a small chance she still somehow remembered that, him cradling the warmth of her tiny body as it howled against the night.

Falling
IN LOVE

THIS HAPPENS TO EVERYONE. It is nothing all that special, despite the fact that you have worn uncomfortable shoes and underwear that gives you a rash. More wine, he offers, pouring without a question mark. The heart is an involuntary muscle, you think to yourself.

His aftershave smells like your father's. You scrape your face against the stubble of his beard and wonder if the little hairs from his razor are still in the bathroom sink where he left them, bleeding from his chin then and already late to meet you at the expensive restaurant where you sat crossing and uncrossing your silk-stockinged legs, wondering if you would be able to find a 24-hour drugstore that sold Vagisil. He panted his apology, you with one arm already in your good wool coat, and you saw the wrinkles between his eyes. Yes, yes of course you would stay and have a glass of wine, a nice meal, with the man whose cheek, when it brushed against yours, sharp but not unkind, reminded you of climbing into the rope hammock, your father folding his newspaper and saying, Well there's my girl, him playing with your hair as you listened to the strange smallness of his heartbeat.

Would you like to come in? followed dinner, dessert, coffee that came in a tall glass with a long silver spoon. There were thirty-two steps up to his apartment, each one crooked, the grey enamel worn by the generations of transient footsteps carved into the staircase. More wine, he says again now, the point being that there are too many obstacles to your leaving. Your teeth already blackened with tannins. Your lips stained.

You met him at a party where it was easy to smile, your lip gloss shining and your hair flat-ironed, everything about you smooth. Anyone special in your life? he asked, but it was difficult to take him seriously in his tuxedo shirt with "Year 2000" suspenders, the implication being that both of you should party like it was 1999, the joke made several times, the realization dawning that you had promised yourself at midnight of the new millennium, drunk and throwing up into a punch bowl, that within five years you would be somebody's wife. You would have a car, a dog. A baby. You thought about sleeping late on Sundays and making him coffee the way he liked it and never again wearing the underwear that cut between your legs while making your bum look so small and shapely. You saw yourself eating Chinese food in bed. Him teaching you how to use chopsticks, you getting rice all over your nightshirt, the two of you falling asleep with greasy mouths of unbrushed teeth. That is love, you thought. The kind of love that tastes like sweet and sour pork. Of tart, sticky fruit.

The bottle of wine is almost empty and you have had enough dates with him to know that soon he will bite your lip, stand you up and press you against the wall. You on the tiptoes of one foot, the other leg wrapped around him, solely for balance. And because you tell yourself you are in love, you might let him flip you over on the bed, the fingernail of his left thumb sharp and cutting as he pushes inside you, the other hand grabbing your hip bone like it was a haunch. You will whimper just like your best-friend-forever Marie taught you to when you practiced French kissing in her bedroom. Rolling on the unicorn bedspread. Touching the mohair blanket. Velvet teddy bears. Eighth-grade breasts. Until she whimpered.

No, no, it's fine—guys like it when they can't tell if you're gonna cry or if you're gonna come.

The two of you in prom dresses, drunk on the hood of the car your dates had rented, the boys getting high behind the sports equipment bunker as you soaked in the orange light of the parking lot, shining. Marie's finger traced the path of your blood as it shuddered back to your heart, your skin a fire she had helped dress. Your hands on her shoulders, her arms open, fanning out the silky fabric you stepped into like the promise of a second skin. Her mother gave you a beer while you did each other's make-up and said, smoothing your blush, God, you'll never be younger than you are right now. She curled your hair and gave both of you emergency money, twenty dollars she made you safety pin inside your bras.

Marie taught you how to ride a bike in the city. She rode ahead of you, your eyes drawn to the flashing red light on her backpack as you remembered your father in the parking lot of the Catholic school, lying to you as you wobbled away: I've still got you, I've still got you. Marie's skirt tucked between her legs and your hands cramping in the cold as you made your way to Mike Willis' party, the Freshman Fiesta, which Marie called the Freshman Fuckfest. You were invited because Marie was invited. Because Marie invited you. You got off your bikes and chained them to a No Parking sign, and Marie, a slight blurriness to her edges, had tears from the wind freezing to her cheeks. Her eyes were blue like the Indian Ocean, water you had never seen from across the world. The air between you misty from your breath, you thought she might say that she had not forgotten the gift of your grandmother's bracelet, the thin silver bangle you never took off, for her nineteenth birthday. That she was sorry, somehow. But she just smoothed her skirt and reapplied her lip gloss, swigging from the bottle of gin she dug out of her backpack before she said, God, are we desperate or what?

You saw her again at your high school reunion and met her husband, Thomas, who sells radio air time to companies advertising weight loss products. How did you two know each other? Thomas asked, the question in your arms as you hugged her. Her softness, the warmth of it, startled you—Jennifer, Kaleigh, and Martin, she said, opening her wallet to show you the pictures. She was drinking club soda with lime because she was trying to get pregnant again. She might be pregnant now, Thomas said, patting Marie's stubborn belly with the hand that didn't hold his glass of whisky. Her hair was thick and lustrous, her fingernail beds deep pink. Anyone special in your life? Marie asked in a chit-chat voice as she sipped at her straw, and you saw the dark blood inside of her, pooling in the space between her hip bones, hot and vaguely dangerous as it nourished the unspoken needs of another person who did not yet exist.

And your mother, hanging laundry in early spring. Her hands chapped and red against the green of new grass, the white of bleached sheets. You're too young to have a boy-friend, honey (you holding the basket and the clothespins, wishing for mittens). But don't worry, when you're old enough, you'll find somebody. It happens to everyone. Your mother, humming a song, here and there saying the words, Hearts and bones, hearts and bones.

The danger is this: the walls of your heart will become thinner and thinner until there is nothing left but a void, the size and shape of which you recognize in the same way you know your own face, looking in a mirror.

TICK

THIRTEEN SECONDS is about as long as it takes to settle into the driver's seat of your car, buckle up your seatbelt, and turn the key in the ignition. It's about as long as it takes to eat three french fries, if you're eating them one by one. It's about as long as it takes to carry a bag of garbage to the curb from your front door.

Thirteen seconds is the average amount of time the average person spends washing his or her hands after using the bathroom. Please keep in mind that the average person's hands are, on average, laden with bacteria that can be deadly to the very young, the very old, and those with immunodeficiency conditions. Thirteen seconds is not enough time to kill deadly bathroom germs. This is why there has been a nationwide campaign promoting good handwashing practices. Perhaps you've seen the posters? "Don't be Dirty—Count to Thirty."

It takes fewer than thirteen seconds to say this: "The chief problem with being a moral individual is the fact that we live in an amoral universe." It may be helpful to adopt this perspective as you read the rest of the story.

Perspective is all about looking: who is doing the looking, and who is being looked at. Who is the seer, and who or what is the seen object? This kind of narrative theory sounds simple, but it can get tricky. Sometimes it can pose very serious problems for very serious students—students who are interested in getting it right. In the interest of helping out these scholars, should they happen to be reading, here's a hint: for the most part, you and I will be doing the looking, and the object we will occasionally be looking at is Franklin Murdoch in the last thirteen seconds of his life.

Tick Tick

MORNING BROKE with a snap of fiery sunrise that felt like the sting of an elastic band. The members of the firing party, standing fifteen paces away from the post, their backs turned, were from Franklin's own battalion. Each man was busy trying to pretend that his rifle was the lucky one the officer in charge had loaded with the blank. That way, each man reasoned, his rifle was just a noisemaker, as harmless as a party cracker at a child's birthday. There was a little white circle of paper pinned to Franklin's chest. Shining.

The Assistant Provost Marshal was there, pleased with himself for organizing the festivities. Franklin's NCO was there, too, looking constipated. There was an officer, petting his pistol like it was a teacup poodle, and a sergeant there just for fun—he didn't even get to shoot anybody. He was an invitee by obligation only. Everybody was there. It was a regular blowout.

And Franklin was there, too.

Franklin handed over his identification and his pay book to the NCO who said in a gravelly voice, "Yep, this is Murdoch. Deserter Extraordinaire."

There was a stretcher, in case Franklin couldn't make it to the post on his own two legs. He didn't need it, though. Franklin was no coward, despite all evidence to the contrary. He kept his eyes wide open as the blindfold was tied.

You show up just as the last knot is cinched.

Good timing, and welcome.

Now that there are more guests, Franklin gets into the spirit of his own party. In a low voice, sweet and warm, he starts to sing. Unbeknownst to any of the other party-goers, the fragmented song he sings will resurface in the mouth of a 1960s travelling-troubadour-folk-singer who some people—people high on drugs, naturally—will think is Jesus Christ, reborn.

"'Twas in another lifetime, one of toil and blood, when blackness was a virtue, and the road was full of mud . . . in a world of steel-eyed death, and men who are fighting to be warm . . . I bargained for salvation an' they gave me a lethal dose . . ."

The song will be recorded in September 1974 and become part of an album released by Columbia Records to mixed reviews in mid-January 1975. The songs will be about love and pain, love and pain, and the album title will have something to do with blood and railroads. Eventually it will be considered one of the greatest albums of all time. Franklin, if not for the unpleasantness he currently finds himself embroiled in, would first hear the song on a rainy February evening. Franklin, then seventy-six years old with arteriosclerosis and erectile dysfunction, would hear the song on his eldest grandchild's record player and proceed to scream bloody murder: who was that curly-haired bastard who stole his song, the one he wrote in the war? But Franklin, if all this happens, will be a war veteran, the kind people make allowances for. Don't worry about him, his grandson will tell his friends as the record spins. My granddad's kind of crazy.

Luckily we won't have to worry about any of that. The NCO has seen to it, though the singing is starting to piss him off. The APM is all shook up (wahoo hoo, hoo, hey, hey, yeah, yeah). The riflemen are unnerved. The medical officer wishes that he had sedated Franklin. The sergeant is worried: all the singing is bad for morale. Even Franklin knows he is burning up a lot of 4/4 time. You and I, though, we like the song. We just sit back and listen.

Tick Tick Tick

A LITTLE WHILE AGO, Franklin Murdoch had two thousand, seven hundred and fourteen seconds left. This is a number considerably greater than thirteen, but not any more pleasing an amount—not from Franklin Murdoch's point of view, anyhow. It was an important moment in time, nonetheless: it was then that Franklin finally got an audience with God.

God had been rather difficult to get in touch with lately. In fact, He'd been totally incommunicado. God, Franklin reasoned, was obviously very busy with the war. Besides, everyone, no matter how omniscient, needs a break now and again. A recent study indicates that overworked employees are less productive, and you can't argue with that.

"Our Father, who art in heaven, hallowed be Thy name..." Franklin was confident that God would come through this time. Why, not that long ago (...Thy kingdom come, Thy will be done...) Franklin had put his hands over the bloody

slop of Conway's arm that was not really there anymore (...
on earth as it is in heaven ...) and Conway had screamed
"Holy Jesus, Goddamn Motherfucker, Holy Christ! Mother-
fucking Mary, Mother of God!" (... give us this day ...) and
the blood and the sharp bone and the gristle of fat and
stringy muscles and tendons had stuck to Franklin's own
arm—which was still there, Franklin was pretty sure, and
thank God for that!—in a soupy paste of meat (... our daily
bread ...) and gore, and he had seen Conway's eyes roll back
into his head (... forgive us our trespasses ...), even as Conway still shouted out "Jesus Christ, you Goddamn Motherfucker!" (... as we forgive those who trespass against us ...),
and in the end Conway cried as the medic had prepared to
amputate (... lead us not into temptation ...) and Murdoch
looked on bravely (... but deliver us from evil ...) and was
given some sort of medal or ribbon for his part in the whole
mess (... for Thine is the kingdom, and the power, and the
glory, for ever and ever ...), and even now he could still hear
Conway crying like a baby that he didn't want to die; and
please, God, he didn't want to die (... Amen).

Out of the disorienting eddy of blood and dirt and shells
and fucks and oh shits, God managed not only to hear Conway's obscenity-laden prayer, but also to answer it and save
his life. Nothing could be done about the arm. God is a
miracle-worker, not a magician. At least Conway still had
his life, thanks to God. No other explanation for it, really,
the medical men said. A goddamn miracle.

So Franklin Murdoch prayed in his own little hour of
need. He was hopeful and his cell was quiet: there wasn't
nearly as much noise to filter out as there had been when
Conway was calling Jesus a motherfucker. Franklin reasoned
that his prayer was probably going straight through to God,

loud and clear. Plus, a ribbon, or a medal, whatever it was, should count for something, too. And the fact that he didn't use foul language, that should also help his cause, Franklin thought.

"Sincerely, your humble servant, Franklin Murdoch."

With two thousand, seven hundred and fourteen seconds to go, Franklin opened his eyes, looked down, and saw between his feet a Chinese fortune cookie.

It was an impossibility. It had no business being in the spartan cell, yet it was there. It was a beautiful tawny half-moon of salvation. Franklin instantly forgot about the cigarettes and the bottle of brandy. He turned away from his last meal of dry potatoes and lumpy gravy. The fortune cookie had appeared to him in that desert of deserts, appeared out of nothing as a sign. It was a one hundred percent, reliable, certifiable, goddamn miracle.

Franklin gently picked up his crunchy, sugary little marvel, cradling it in both hands as though it was a little piece of God, Himself.

"Thank you, God," Franklin said, and then he cracked open the cookie to read aloud its message of deliverance.

"Confucius say: Never eats an any thing bigger than you head."

He now had two thousand, six hundred and seven seconds left, and in the passing of that one minute and forty-seven seconds, Franklin Murdoch, if he was paying attention, had learned this: God was letting a lot of things slide, including the quality of English language translations from the Wong Phat Fortune Cookie Company of Qinghai, China.

Tick Tick

POOR FRANKLIN. It really is a shame, if you stand back and take in the whole picture. He is tall and still, his face and hands very white and almost waxy. Except for the bloated clouds of condensation coming out of his mouth as he sings the last few notes, you'd think he was dead, or at least that he was an escapee from Madame Tussaud's. But that is not the case. We already know what kind of escapee Franklin is.

My goodness, though, doesn't he look waxy? Those men holding the guns should save their bullets and just put a wick in Franklin and let him quietly burn himself out. But then where would the fun be in that? And those gun-holding men do look awfully smart in their uniforms; too bad Franklin is blindfolded. Someone is whispering orders and the men are raising their rifles. Their mothers, I'm sure, are very proud.

Maybe Franklin's skin just knows that he is going to die in about five seconds, and it's trying the whole "death thing" out, seeing if it can play the part convincingly. That way, when it comes time to turn Franklin's story into a summer blockbuster, Skin can play Itself and make enough money to officially retire from the daily sweating-stinking-breathing-shedding-healing-containing that is its nine-to-five (and to-nine-again) job.

Or maybe Franklin is already dead—the life sucked out of him by something other than a speeding bullet. In case you haven't guessed, Franklin is no Superman. He is very, very average. One can safely assume that his hands are rife with bacteria.

There's nothing I can do. I'm only following orders.

I was very clear on that.

If I could be responsible for Franklin, I'd treat him right. I'd send him on a Carnival Cruise until his nerves settled, and maybe give him a week or so at Disneyland. There ain't nothin' that cures the blues better than a few trips around Space Mountain. I'd let him drive fast cars and get him even faster women. I'd let him fuck them on the first date and not even make him pay for dinner. I'd give him a job as a proof-reader at a publishing house. Imagine it: each day Franklin loses himself in any number of fictional worlds, looking for errors. If he finds any, he fixes them. Those worlds become error-free.

But I'm already helping Franklin out. Without me, he wouldn't even have been resurrected for these thirteen seconds. And he knew right from the beginning what he was getting himself into. No matter what, though, I'm still not responsible for all of this. It's no mistake that Franklin is standing here as the sun shines, struggling now to come out from behind leaden clouds and a black shroud of mist—it's his own fault he's here, blindfolded; that's what the Field General Courts-Martial concluded.

Don't shoot the messenger.

Tick Tick

FIVE MILLION, three hundred and ninety-nine thousand, one hundred and fourteen seconds ago, Franklin Murdoch was somewhere else entirely. I can't tell you where, exactly—that is Classified Information. I know that's frustrating, but believe me, it's an absolutely vital matter of National Secu-rity. Plus, if I tell you anything more, it won't get through the censors, and who knows what will happen to me if I try? He was walking, I can tell you that, but I can't tell you where from, or where to.

He was imagining a huge meal—a plate of bloody roast beef dripping in gravy, caressed by mashed potatoes, kissed lightly by green peas. He saw squash blushing an embarrassed orange as he brought it to his glistening lips. Pink filling from a strawberry-rhubarb pie, steaming, oozed onto the delicate white plate. It was a meal, Gentle Reader, that was obviously much bigger than his head. In that moment the foodstuffs in Franklin's mind were so real, he felt that he could taste them with the whole of his skinny, sagging, painful, sorry being.

Franklin stopped walking. He looked down at his hands, which were downright filthy. He unshouldered his gun and placed it carefully on the ground. He wiped his hands on his pants. Then, very slowly, he turned around and started walking in the opposite direction.

I can't tell you which direction that was either (see above), but believe me, it was a dangerous direction—more dangerous than the original direction, even considering that the original direction had far more bullets and explosions and scared and angry people than the one Franklin actually chose. Again, I can't tell you exactly where the new direction took him, but I can tell you this: the new direction led exactly to where he is now.

Tick

FICTION does funny things to people. People like you and me, for example. If we met in real life, we'd chat over coffee and have ourselves a perfectly charming afternoon. But since we're meeting on the page, things are different. We are implied. I am the implied author and you are the implied reader. We have been transformed into narrative masks. Franklin wears a mask—a blindfold. I bet you a dollar that he doesn't give a damn about any mask other than that one.

I know I can come on a bit strong. You can feel me every-where in this story; I refuse to blend into the background, or hide behind a coat rack, or a flower arrangement, or a post stuck in the ground, or a little circular piece of white paper, for that matter. So out of fairness, I figure if you can feel me, I should let Franklin feel me, too. Give him a good feel of a real red-blooded girl before these next seconds pass. Franklin is an okay guy. You'd know that if I had told you more about him. Who knows? Maybe I'd have let him get more than just a feel, if things had been different. I'm a sucker for a man in uniform. And I think it's important to support the troops.

I'm sorry if you haven't had fun. I know that a good story is supposed to have a beginning, a middle, and an end. This story only has thirteen seconds. It's also well known that if a story is to be a tragedy, it must be of a certain amplitude. Very shortly, Franklin will have no amplitude. He will be flatline. Besides, a tragedy must represent something that is worthy of our serious attention as readers, and let's be honest: no one cares about Franklin, and this story is about handwashing, large meals, time, and waxiness.

But time marches on, and everybody loves a parade. Franklin has a few seconds left. That should be enough. You came here to be entertained, and there is a spectacle to see. It was nice to meet you. Open your eyes.

Tick

Tick

Way Back THE ROAD

"**D**EATH IS A GREEDY THING," Uncle Joseph said, "like a cat starving its way through winter. It don't need your help to kill you." Luke sat cross-legged on the floor in his best pair of corduroys and took a drink of the warm Coke Aunt Louise had poured for him. The Vaseline from his fat lip left a trail of slime on the rim of the glass. He already knew that death could sneak up at any moment, like it did to the Guitar boys, their pink lungs filling with black pond water in the thaw just before Christmas. The paper had put their school pictures on the front page and Luke's mother had cut out the clipping and Scotch-taped it to the fridge, saying, "You hold onto that railing, Luke. Things happen just like that." She snapped her fingers and Luke had felt them pinching at his heart.

"You hearing me, Luke?"

"You shut your mouth, Joseph," Louise said. "We don't need more talk."

Luke was pretty sure that Aunt Louise knew a thing or two about death, but she was a little fragile now, his mother said. One day Uncle Maurice was baiting the traps with horse meat, and the next he was lying in a box wearing a tie, bought special. Louise had nearly gone deaf from the shock of it all. Luke remembered that when the news came she had asked the person on the other end to repeat himself before letting out a little cry, one like the minks sometimes made when the metal door slammed, and then her mouth had gone slack and she had hit the receiver with the heel of her hand. "Believe this, Ferne? Phone's busted again," she said, her lips still moving after the end of the words. She had held the phone out even as Luke heard the chief of police shouting, "Lou, are you still there, did you hear me? I'm sorry."

His mother explained that it was just nature's way. "People can go a bit loopy when bad things happen," she said. "It's normal."

Louise had kissed the cheek of her dead husband at the funeral, her new hearing aids buzzing the whole time, and the powder blush had stuck to her lipstick, making her look like she'd eaten a pink sugar donut. Uncle Maurice was the first dead body Luke had ever seen and he had been afraid to do what the men did, what his father did: stand solemnly at the casket and put one warm, live hand on top of Maurice's white, dead one. "It's just a hand," his mother said in an irritated voice, loud enough for Father Richard to hear.

But Luke was older now and he knew better than to act like a baby at these things, especially now that Shel was here, testing the open bottles on the tables and stealing swigs from the ones with little bits left. It didn't look like Cynthia was coming and Shel was worse without her. Luke had to be careful.

He took a sip of his Coke and wished it were cold so he could press it against his lip; his mother said that would take down the bruise, even after the fact. Luke looked around the room for her. Mr. Ducharme was saying that his gravel business was going to make him rich in five years, and Mrs. Robichaud smoked a cigarette, telling people between puffs to shut their yaps so she could hear the baby crying. Luke wanted to go home.

"You staying out of trouble there, tough guy?" Doris Charette was old and smelled like rotten cherries and baby powder, but Luke liked her anyway. His dad said that Doris had a head stuffed full of nothing but air and the recipe for Jell-O, but she was the only person who didn't mind if Luke used swear words or ran around in the cold without his jacket, trying to catch his death. If he wanted an answer, Doris might give him one, even though he knew it was a mistake to keep asking. His father had said as much when Luke tried him, sitting on his parents' bed and watching him curse at his tie. "You ask again, Luke, and you'll feel a bit a hell from me," he had said.

"You get something to eat, Lukie?"

"Doris," he said, "is Martin going to hell?"

"Jesus, Luke." Her eyes went over him like a garden rake. She didn't say anything else as she sat down beside him and took a sip from his glass.

"It's warm," she said. "And flat."

"I'm sorry."

"You been talking to Shel and them?"

"No," Luke lied.

"Well don't," Doris said. "He's thirteen going on idiot."

She took another sip as Paul Cowley came down the stairs and the room got quiet with trailed-off conversation.

Mr. Cowley slowed as he waded through people's stares. Luke looked at the floor but worried that might be impolite. Where was his mother?

Mr. Cowley's eyes were red from crying, but they tended to be red anyway, or at least pink most of the time. He was allergic to dust and pollen and all sorts of things—shellfish, Luke thought, and maybe peanuts, too—and sometimes in the spring, right around the time when the fiddleheads were out, he wore goggles around town, and thin cotton gloves. Once Luke had seen him in the window of The Waterside having a beer after work and looking like a starving robot with metallic eyes and harsh cheekbones. The hands of a ghost.

Mr. Cowley and Luke's father both worked in heating and cooling, and so sometimes Mr. and Mrs. Cowley came over for dinner. Martin was in high school, old enough to stay home alone. Luke was allowed to eat in the basement and watch a movie, something that wasn't too violent and didn't show bare breasts or use the f-word, not that anyone came down to check. His mother was too busy fretting about the dinner, even though she almost always served Shake 'n Bake chicken, and that was hard to screw up. It wasn't fancy, she said, but it was safe. Nobody was allergic to Shake 'n Bake.

Paul Cowley stood on the bottom stair. "There's more whisky in the cupboard," he said loudly. He came to sit beside Uncle Joseph who hung one arm around his neck and shoulders like a scarf on a scarecrow.

"I'm going up to check on Maryanne. I told Paul to give her something," Doris said, heaving herself up. "We'll talk later. Just don't you listen to Shel, okay?"

Why did people tell him that all the time? Did they sit around thinking that he was hanging off Shel's every word, following him around the schoolyard and just hoping to get slaughtered? Luke wasn't stupid, one fat lip was enough. But he couldn't keep avoiding Shel forever, not when there was only one way across the pond to school and that was right in his territory, from the bottom of the hill near the culvert to the chain link fence around the back field.

Shel had parked himself there in the middle of the bridge on the first day back after the holidays, jumping on the steps to splinter the wood while Cynthia stood around in a too-small ski parka that showed her wrists and her belly.

"Hey, Luke," Shel had shouted between jumps. "You hear about Sam Purdin's dog?"

"What about him?"

"Her," Cynthia said. She sat down on the middle step and hugged her ankles. She put her chin on her knees and looked back across the field, chapping her lips with her tongue.

"What?"

"Her. It's a girl. The dog."

"A bitch," Shel said.

Luke crossed his arms. His father said he needed to stand up for himself. Shel was nothing more than a bag of hot air who needed a haircut.

"She found Martin Cowley," Shel said as he hacked at the step with the heel of his boot.

Luke knew that Martin drove around town in an old Honda, one elbow hanging out the window even in the dead of winter, but that was about it. Martin had played Joseph in the Christmas pageant the year that Luke was a talking sheep, back when Luke's mother still insisted they all go to church, at least around Christmas. His parents sat with the Cowleys, close enough for Luke to see Maryanne Cowley mouth Martin's lines along with him. The only thing Luke had ever said to him was, "Behold the Christmas star."

"What are you talking about?"

"She found him. Dog yapped her bloody face off and wouldn't come back from the woods," Shel said. He hurled a piece of wood into the water. "When Sam went to get her, there was Martin, stretching his neck, if you follow." Shel mimed wrapping a rope around his neck, putting one arm in the air and pretending to dangle from it, his tongue out and waggling at Cynthia who gave him the finger.

Luke shrugged. "I'm going to be late for school," he said. Shel made stuff up all the time.

"You an idiot? Don't you get it?"

He didn't. That was the kind of thing you saw in R-rated movies about people living in New York or Los Angeles. People didn't do it in real life. Besides, Martin had had a solo in the pageant, the line in "Away in a Manger" about loving Jesus forever and staying by his side. Shel was the idiot.

"You're lying."

"The fuck I am."

"I'm going to be late," Luke said again. All he had to do was go to class and ask Mrs. Solomon about it. He knew what she was going to say: No, Luke, and you can't believe everything you see on TV, either. When his mom found out she might have half a mind to go over and tell Jeanette just what kind of foul things came out of her boy's dirt mouth, but his dad would say, C'mon Ferne, and put an end to that. It was all fine. This was just Shel being Shel. A bad egg, his mother said.

"You piss yourself when you get strangled, you know." Shel wiped a hand over his mouth. "Your tongue turns purple and your eyes break all their blood vessels while you struggle, but there's nothing you can do about it once you jump." He put his hands around his own throat and made choking noises, and Luke remembered the time he'd cut himself with his mother's very sharp kitchen knife. The damage done before the quick blossoming of blood. The second before the pain.

"Dog got a hold of his foot and wouldn't let go, taste a death and all that," Shel went on. "Paul Cowley eventually had to beat the bitch off with a broom handle and she wound up losing her puppies. Sam Purdin should sue for loss a property."

"You don't know shit." Cynthia stood and hiked up her jeans, hugging herself against the cold.

"I know that Martin's going to get buried at the crossroads way back the road so his soul can never find its way," Shel said. "They'll bury him standing upside-down and they'll put a stake in his heart on account of his being a suicide."

Cynthia rolled her eyes and brushed the bangs off her face.

"And I heard that he did it because he's a faggot." Shel kicked the posts of the bridge. "Was a faggot, I mean. Fucking disgusting."

"Not everyone's a fag, you know," Cynthia said as she pulled at the cuffs of her jacket.

"Take Luko, over there. A faggot if I ever saw one."

Luke stood there feeling small and stupid as Shel and Cynthia both looked him over.

"Did your mommy make you wear that hat, Luke?" Shel said. "Do you suck your daddy's dick?"

"Grow up, Shel," Cynthia said, picking up her backpack. "I'm going to school."

"Bitch." Shel turned back to Luke as Cynthia started over the bridge. "Hey faggot, you checking me out?"

All Luke had to do was run. What was Shel going to do, belt him in the face as he ran by? Shel was just going to laugh and call Luke a pussy and throw an ice ball at his head, and Cynthia was still there, not that far ahead.

"You gonna stand there and whack off to me?"

Luke was fast. And small. These were good things. He just had to do it. Stand up for himself.

Shel grabbed his crotch. "I got something you want, faggot?"

Luke's forehead caught Shel in the chest. There was no sound except for the hollow thud of body hitting body, the salty wool of Shel's jacket crashing into Luke's open mouth. Shel with one heel dug into the bridge, then Shel floating over the water, a magic boy, a look on his face like he wanted to say something, that he was sorry, maybe, before the water filled his lungs and bathed his eyes, still open, turning him into something cold and new, a picture on a piece of newsprint on the fridge door, curling and fading from the heat of the stove.

It hadn't mattered that Luke heard Shel clawing his way out of the pond, slapping his sopping jacket on the ground and yelling that Luke was going to fucking die when he got his fucking hands on him, fucking die. Luke had run, the weight of his own soul slowing him down in the deep, wet snow. He knew what had happened, the thought repeating in his mind: You killed Shel, you killed Shel. The taste of the unsaid words a lot like blood.

After that it had been a relief to go to the cemetery and see the hole, the tracks from the backhoe in the newly softened ground. Luke thanked his lucky stars he hadn't asked anyone, not even Doris, about burying Martin upside-down at the crossroads, even though he still almost wished he had seen the body in the coffin, just so he could be sure of things before he threw his own handful of earth on the empty-sounding lid. Wharton's funeral home had kept the casket closed the whole time. They put a giant picture of Martin on an easel, which his mother said was a small mercy, although Luke wasn't sure why. Father Richard had prayed over the coffin before it was lowered into the ground, but that didn't mean that the thing about Martin's soul couldn't still be true. Shel lied, but not about everything. Luke had sat between his parents during the service, conscious of the fact that he had no brothers and sisters. If Shel killed him, his parents were going to be alone in the world. If his parents died, the same was true for him.

Martin had a brother. John worked for a gas company and was exploring somewhere near Baffin Island. Although they hadn't been able to reach him yet, the company planned on doing everything they could for the Cowley family during this trying time, including transferring John back home for a month or two, if need be. It was hard to guess how Mr. and Mrs. Cowley felt about that—if it was more of a comfort to have a son not there, not in a box, a son who spent his time scaling mountains and drilling into the ground and being alive, or if it was a strange torture to have their only other boy out in God knows where with nothing between him and Martin but miles and time and luck and a length of sturdy, splintered rope. Luke sipped his Coke and understood a bit better why his own mother had insisted on holding his hand while Father Richard talked about ashes to ashes, her finger-nails digging into his skin.

Luke walked over to the window, keeping an eye out for Shel. Luke's father was smoking on the porch with Uncle Joseph and Paul Cowley. They stood in a silent triangle and Luke watched the air float out of their mouths and fill the dark between them with gauzy, hot smoke. His father looked tall and strong, his space in the night brightened by a single glowing spark, fuelled by his own hazy breath.

If Luke got his mother her coat, maybe she would take him home; he wasn't allowed to walk alone at night, which was fine by Luke. The dark made him nervous. She was more than likely fixing coffee with Doris in the kitchen, trying to get the pot off before people started searching for their jackets and jingling their keys, slurring things about it being late and needing to get back. There was always the chance his father might come too if he was finished with his cigarette, or if his mother kissed him on the cheek and said, It's getting on, Jim. His parents loved each other like that. He had seen the photo his mother hid in the kitchen cupboard, the one where her hair was long and wavy as she looked over her shoulder and the small strap of her nightgown slid down her arm, his father taking the picture.

The coats were heaped on a bed upstairs. John's old bed-room, not Martin's, Luke hoped as he came up to the door with the hand-lettered sign that said, Keep Out, That Means You Mom. Luke couldn't find the light switch but it didn't matter. He knew the feel of his mother's jacket, the collar a gift from Uncle Maurice, the smell of her in the fur now. But there was another smell in the room. Something punky, like an apple left on a radiator.

"Shut the door."

Luke's heart beat in his ears and eyes and brain, and the thought of running downstairs and calling for his mother, his father, Doris, even, was stopped by the hammering of blood. There was nothing to be done. He had been stupid and now he was going to pay for it.

"Come over here." Shel was sitting on the floor at the end of the bed, his head on his knees. The triangle of yellow light from the bulb in the hallway showed Luke the back of Shel's neck, pale and shiny. "You got cigarettes?" Shel asked.

"No," Luke said.

"Course you don't." Shel slugged a nearly empty wine bottle to his lips.

Luke saw the piles of sick on the floor. There was some on the edge of the ruffled bed skirt and some in a puddle between Shel's knees where he sat horking, his spit making a thwacking noise when it hit the mess.

"You sick or something?" Luke breathed through his mouth as he came closer. "Shel?"

"I told her I would pay for it," Shel said into the floor. "I can get the money. You think I can't get the money? Bitch." He spat again. "Fucking bitch."

Luke jumped as Shel gave a spastic hiccup. Shel wretched between his legs and then sipped from the bottle, choking down the wine until he heaved again, his fist pounding the carpet with each rush of his insides. Luke didn't know what to think, only that he wished Shel would just snap out of it and tell him that he was going to punch his lights out. Instead he swayed back and forth on the carpet like a Boy Scout at a make-believe campfire.

"She said I'm going to hell because a this. Her too." Shel's tongue sounded fat in his mouth.

"We should go." Luke's eyes were adjusting to the dark and he saw that Shel's lips were stained and chewed up, his teeth working at a small flap of skin in the corner that was starting to bleed. He could imagine what Mrs. Cowley was going to say about blood on the carpet and the piles of puke. "This might be Martin's room."

Shel wiped a hand over his mouth, smearing some blood onto his cheek. He crawled onto his knees, grinding the vomit into the floor as he steadied himself. "Are you disrespecting the dead?" Shel dragged out the d-sounds, running his free hand over the lump of jackets on the bed, then stamping the bottle on his palm as he wobbled closer. He breathed heavily and squinted at Luke until his eyes were nothing more than sticky slivers.

There was music playing downstairs and people laughing as Shel stared at Luke and thumped the bottle in his hand.

"I'm sorry about the bridge, Shel," Luke said. He didn't know why, only that he meant it.

"You don't fucking know from sorry." Shel's eyes were nearly swollen shut. "They're not even going to bury it, you know." He pawed the bottle at Luke. "She told me they're just going to scrape it out and put it in a bag and then burn it like garbage, like it didn't even have a soul."

"What are you talking about?"

"Fucking garbage."

Shel swung the bottle in a wild and lazy arc that caught the corner post of Martin's bed. He fell hard onto his knees like they weren't his anymore, like he had deflated from the inside out and was now just the skin and bone outline of a dead boy. It was over, whatever had happened, and Luke was safe, absolved, only a witness to the strange and secret ritual that had Shel hunched over and curled around the bottle, begging for forgiveness. This was suffering, Luke knew. This was grace. Then the room flared up. Paul Cowley. He was in the doorway, hand on the light switch. Luke stood there, blinking, his elbows locked and his fists sweaty.

Mr. Cowley took a step into the room and when he saw Shel in a ball and the stains on the carpet, he rubbed at one eye and the white of it went bloodshot.

"Shel?"

Shel's head lolled back and his eyes rolled around, seeing everything and nothing.

"You clean your mess," Mr. Cowley said. "Then you get yourself gone."

Shel burped. Paul Cowley rubbed at his eye again and made to leave, half turning to look at Luke.

"Your parents are staying for a bit. Your dad said you can walk home if you want."

Luke watched him leave the room before he found his coat and zipped it up, tying his scarf tight as Shel moaned and covered his eyes with his arm. Luke promised himself he wasn't going to be afraid. He was just going to have to be careful. It wasn't that far home.

The
VOSMAK GENEALOGY

MY MOTHER HAD NO IMAGINATION. She said her condition was an unusual form of brain damage caused by an accident that happened at her parents' annual First Day of Spring Party in March, 1956.

Though my mother's parents had been born in Toronto, as had their parents before them, both my grandmother and grandfather claimed to have a memory of the seasons of their homeland, the location of which they disputed. My grandfather was adamant that the family came from Koryakia, while my grandmother swore they were actually from Magadan. The possibility that my grandmother and grandfather might come from different places was never raised. For my grandparents, marriage fused histories in the same way it joined destinies.

"Your grandfather wouldn't know his homeland if it sat down and had a drink with him," my grandmother said in Russian, leading me around by the wrist while we shopped for *kovbasa* at Mike's Meats. Likewise, my grandfather, rolling cigarettes at the kitchen table, said my grandmother couldn't be trusted on this matter. "Sure," he said in English. "That woman couldn't find Russia on a map of Russia." To my knowledge, neither of them ever went any farther east than Montreal, and only then to a lung specialist who told my grandfather that there was nothing to be done about his dying. When it came to their origins, the one thing my grandparents could agree on was the issue of weather. The weather there, in Koryakia or Magadan, was tediously the same, different across the year only in the sense that one month might be slightly less cold than the month before, or the sun a little longer in the sky. The weather in Canada, and Toronto in particular, was a wondrous variety—vibrant budding, heat so flat it made you sleepy, storms that turned sky the black of rotten fruit. Though they were not literary or philosophical people, my grandparents understood Toronto weather as a metaphor for life. It was the inevitability of change they enjoyed. It gave them comfort, I think. They were not religious but they believed in celebrating their blessings, and this meant that every equinox and solstice, or the closest Sunday after, they packed up the family and headed to Grenadier Pond for a picnic.

At the winter parties my mother and her siblings, two sickly twin sisters and one fat little brother, skated until their cheeks burned, and my grandmother made them hot chocolate over a small fire, counting out marshmallows according to their ages, one for each year. In the summer there was lemonade, lawn chairs, the roasting of hot dogs that blistered and split, falling into the coals. Even in the fall the children had fun, collecting bouquets of brightly coloured leaves that they presented to their mother, shyly, as though she were a visiting dignitary or magistrate. Their father smoked cigarettes, offering his wife a drag now and again. The spring parties, however, were always miserable.

Usually there was still snow on the ground, and my grandmother's new spring hat, something with a gauzy half veil and artificial flowers, seemed sad against the slush of the parking lot, garish against the white of the shoreline as she marched back and forth, trying to keep warm. While she was out of earshot, my mother's sisters, Eva and Marlene, huddled together and bugged Larry, the spoiled brat, to make a fuss about leaving. But my grandmother insisted that they weren't leaving until they enjoyed their spring picnic, and they should be happy that they were born in the wonderful weather of Toronto and not back in Magadan where it was a thousand times colder and the sun never shone and things were still hard, unbearably hard, because of the war.

"Koryakia," my grandfather said.

On the day of her accident, my mother helped my grandmother spread out rubber tarps and cover them with knit afghans. They smoothed out the linen placemats, arranging them in a circle. They folded the cloth napkins into clams. My grandmother unleashed steam from each insulated foil package. She dished out cabbage rolls and *kovbasa*, potatoes and squash. "Hurry," she said to my grandfather as he passed her the plates. "You like cold sausage?" There was chicken soup from a thermos, chocolate pudding for dessert. There was even a cupcake for Larry, who was picky and despised pudding. My grandmother cajoled everyone into eating, and for a while it seemed as though the picnic might be the only successful First Day of Spring Party in the history of the Vosmak family.

My mother asked to go play. "Yes, of course, be careful," my grandmother said. My grandparents sipped their coffees, my grandfather convincing my grandmother to let him splash a little brandy into her cup. It was not often that they had this kind of tranquility, and certainly a rarity to have it at a First Day of Spring Party. My grandmother worked at Campbell's during tomato season, Christie's the rest of the year. My grandfather worked at Continental Can, the highest-paying factory in North America at the time. Their children all had new shoes, but my grandfather and grandmother were thin and tired. They understood the keen pleasure of a cup of coffee at a picnic, and they were hungry for that pleasure when it presented itself. They sat there thinking about what a beautiful spring day it was, despite the cold. They did not pay much attention to their second youngest, who, at six years old, was very well-behaved. There was simply no reason for them to watch her as she walked up the hill to play with her doll. I don't think you can blame them.

My mother told me what she remembered, which was not much. She said the picnic tables were leaned up against the various trees and covered in ice and snow. She had crawled between one table and a tree trunk, feeling safe and snug and somewhat proud of herself for finding this lookout. Her mother was resting on her elbow and her legs were both out to one side, like she was on a beach. Her father was teaching Larry how to strike a match. Her sisters, giggling for once, were making sodden snow angels.

"It was," she said, "a very happy moment."

My grandmother told me about the noise, which she said was like a tree screaming. It was a horrible shriek of wood on wood, and it made her remember a story from her childhood that she had not thought about in years, a story about hell and the way the devils there cheered when a new soul came to them. Watching that picnic tabletop score the tree trunk as it slid down to her daughter was the worst moment of my grandmother's life. Worse, she said, than seeing the table teeter like a perverse playground on top of my mother, her one wildly shaking boot the only part of her body not smothered and smashed.

"It was the slide," my grandmother said in Russian, ashamed. "When there was still time for it to be my fault."

My grandfather ran towards the sound before he even turned around. He tripped over a thermos and the spilled coffee burned Eva's hand, though it was Marlene who screamed. My grandmother followed him. They fell over and over again as their feet sank through the crystal-fine crust of the melting snow on the hill. My grandmother crushed the flower on her new hat, trying to keep it on her head.

My grandfather reached my mother first. He bent down low and heaved his body under the edge of the tabletop that jutted up slightly like an expectant diving board. Thick ice coated the splintery wood, encasing the table legs, black against the bright sky, in an uneven layer of solid dead weight. The table was like a massive overturned beetle. The skin around my grandfather's eyes went white as he strained. My grandmother threw herself beside him and the two of them pushed, shifting the table several inches. It slid backwards in the snow and caught a corner of my mother's red jacket, tearing the sleeve away from the shoulder. They pushed again until they heard the cracking of bones. The table dipped to one side as my grandmother fell back, crying and slapping at my grandfather as he kept working. "Stop it, stop it," she screamed. "You're killing her." My grandfather called to Eva and Marlene. "Your sister," he yelled as they stumbled up the hill. The four of them tried to lift the table, but the two girls were small for their age and Eva's hand was badly burned. My grandfather screamed as he let the table down gently. Eva and Marlene sat in the snow and cried as they watched him run to the road, his arms wheeling, looking like a drowning man.

Larry was already there, waving his stubby arms at a car as it drove by. The car stopped and Larry ran to the driver's window, my grandfather far behind. Larry, who was not even five years old and too fat for any of his cousins' clothes.

It took a long time for the ambulance to get to the pond. My grandmother waited with her hand on my mother's foot. She tried to keep it still.

The courts concluded that the melting of the snow, combined with my mother's clambering, dislodged the picnic table. It was essentially an accident. But regardless of these natural, unavoidable, and admittedly contributive facts, the judge still found the City of Toronto negligent and ordered it to pay my parents damages, which went towards my mother's care. She suffered a compressed spine, a fractured skull, a concussion, a broken wrist, a dislocated shoulder, deep lacerations to her face that would leave scars, and a punctured lung. Several of her ribs had splintered like chicken bones. Part of her liver had to be removed. The picnic tables should have been chained up, the judge said. "There is no excuse for there not to be chains, considering the tables each weigh several hundred pounds," he went on, "and while it is a tragedy that your daughter suffered, it is a miracle that no other persons, child or adult, have yet found themselves at the mercy of one of these picnic tables." My grandmother cried into a freshly ironed handkerchief. Today if you go to a Toronto city park in winter, you will find that any picnic table leaned up against a tree is chained. The bylaw is the legacy of my mother's injuries, which left her in hospital for the better part of a year, the first half of it in a coma.

She awoke after months of artificial light and intravenous food, but my grandparents' joy was tempered by the discovery that their little girl had become a baby again. My mother had to relearn how to talk. Then walk. Then feed herself. Each new milestone was celebrated with a cake and pictures. "Look," my grandmother said to the nurses, "look at how well our little Anna is doing," and she got out the album to point out pictures of my mother mashing oatmeal into her mouth.

Over time it became clear that the treatments my mother received were extraordinary—there is a significant article about my mother's recovery in *The New England Journal of Medicine*—but they were also expensive. Even with the settlement, my grandparents sold their house and moved into an apartment that forced Eva and Marlene to share a room with Larry, who was instructed to wait in the hallway when his sisters were changing clothes. My mother came home just after her seventh birthday. She had her own room. Nobody complained.

My mother had been a solitary child before the accident. She was content to play with her doll or make up stories for herself while her sisters fought over hairpins and Larry tried to wheedle extra sweets out of my grandmother. As a result of her ability to entertain herself, my mother had been my grandfather's favourite child. "Look at Anna," he said, ruffling her hair as she poured pretend tea for her doll, Marguerite. "See what a good girl she is, what a quiet girl she is." It was as though good and quiet were two halves of some unnamed, indivisible quality that children worthy of love possessed. As I said, he worked very hard.

The accident did not change my mother's nature; she remained a good, quiet girl, but she was unable to occupy herself with the imaginative play that had come so easily to her before. If my grandmother passed her Marguerite, for example, my mother examined the doll as though it were a strange artifact from another culture, the significance of which she couldn't quite determine. She gently passed Marguerite back to my grandmother, respectful of that which she did not comprehend. If my grandfather began a story while he rolled his cigarettes, perhaps something about the family history in Koryakia, and he asked her, "And then, little Anna, what do you think happened to your great-great-grandfather?" Anna, instead of launching into an elaborate story of her own as she had once been fond of doing, simply shrugged her shoulders and said she didn't know. My grandmother and grandfather exchanged looks, but they were just glad to have their Anna back, and this version that walked about blankly, standing confusedly in front of the pictures on the walls, would do.

My mother's inability to think abstractly became much more obvious in school. Her teacher was a slim British woman named Miss White. She was sensitive to my mother's healing process, and she often encouraged her with her schoolwork. "Pull up your socks, Anna," she said to my mother, who wanted to give up on a frustrating math problem. My mother misunderstood. She put down her pencil, stood up from her desk, and pulled up her knee socks. If one of her classmates remarked that it was "raining cats and dogs," my mother rushed to the window in hysterics. Symbols were cryptic for her. My grandmother packed napkin notes in her children's lunches that said, I ♥ you, and I don't think it's hyperbole to say that it broke her heart when my mother asked her to explain it. Even the explanation proved futile. Love is in the abstract, it seems, not the details.

My mother's specialists could not explain the exact nature of her condition. They advised the family to speak to Anna in unambiguous, factual sentences that referenced concrete, physical objects. Even though this manner of speech became natural to the Vosmaks, they understood that something precious had been lost.

"Poor Marguerite," my grandmother said once in a while as she smoothed the doll's hair, which was made from real horsetail. She left it at that.

The best diagnosis of my mother's condition came twenty years later. At the age of twenty-seven, my mother announced at Sunday dinner that she was pregnant by an exterminator who had come to the house and been delayed by a sudden downpour. My mother had invited him to stay for coffee, she explained, and then sex.

My grandmother, in tears, berated herself for this turn of events. During my mother's pregnancy, which was difficult, my grandmother spent hours in the living room, fingering each picture in the yellowing hospital album, saying over and over again, "An exterminator? Such a lack of imagination."

I might put it slightly differently. I might, though biased, suggest that the most generalized—and yet most accurate—description of my mother's condition is this: through no fault of her own, an inability to love.

*   *   *

IF YOU WERE BORN in Canada between 1976 and 1984, and especially if you were born to middle- or upper-class parents who were also white, suburban, between the ages of thirty and forty-five, and if they answered at least "3: Somewhat Important" to a Likert scale survey that asked them to link the answer to the question "How important are books to your child's development and education?" to a five-point rating system, you are probably familiar with the details of my childhood. And not just because we share the homogenous connection of suburban Canadianness, which makes so many childhoods frighteningly similar across the provinces and territories, but rather because your parents were my mother's target market. I was the product.

If you fit the demographic, odds are that you know about my first visit to the dentist, which ended in the bloody extraction of an impacted baby tooth. Or maybe you're familiar with my trip to the zoo and my fear of koalas. Either way, you know me not by my name, Dora, which publishers at the time considered variously boring, ethnic, and unpopular, but by Nora, the name my mother insisted upon, given its similarity to my real name, for the heroine of her children's books.

That my mother became an author is surprising, considering her condition, but whenever she was confronted on that issue, she seemed insulted and said, "The best stories are true." She was difficult to argue with. She wrote the first book shortly after I was born.

We were living in a small one-bedroom apartment on College Street, above a restaurant named El Greco that was run by Mr. and Mrs. Stephanopolous, a childless couple who served cuisine they referred to as Italian with a Greek flair: spaghetti with a feta cheese sauce, calamari panzerotto. The restaurant was not popular, and that suited us just fine.

My mother had very sensitive hearing, and when we moved in she was concerned about the noise of rattling pots or drunken patrons. "Nothing to worry about there," Mr. Stephanopolous said happily. "I only have a few pots." Mr. Stephanopolous had made his fortune in Greece with an inherited olive farm, and the restaurant was more of a diversion in his retirement than anything else. He enjoyed cooking and would have become a chef had his sense of smell not been obliterated by a war injury that almost killed him—a piece of shrapnel to the soft palate. He experimented with fusion cuisine, anxious for customers' honest feedback; if a dish turned out terribly, the meal was on the house. Students from Central Tech came after school and abused the policy, sprawling over the chairs and dumping their backpacks in the doorway while they ordered mountains of lamb and pita and olives, only to return the dishes to the kitchen once they were more than half eaten, but Mr. Stephanopolous was eminently good-natured. He said that his childhood had been hard and hungry. "Feeding children, even insolent ones, makes me feel like I am doing God's work." Even so, he tested the most experimental dishes on the rowdiest, loudest boys, the ones with leather jackets and gold chains who had girlfriends in skin-tight jeans. "Those kinds of boys," he said, drumming his fingers on the counter, "they'll try anything once."

Mrs. Stephanopolous was fat. Her legs were like telephone poles and her feet, shoved into black loafers, lacked ankles and looked like hooves. Mrs. Stephanopolous smelled of bread, vaguely yeasty and warm. To this day when I walk into a bakery, I think of her. She wore a crucifix around her neck that Mr. Stephanopolous had given her for their fortieth wedding anniversary, and when she was nervous she squeezed it in her fist. If ever I cried for too long, she knocked gently on the apartment door and asked my mother if she would like some help. It's not that my wailing bothered her. She simply wanted an excuse to hold a baby in her arms. Mrs. Stephanopolous carried me around our apartment, chattering away to me in Greek while my mother slept or did dishes and Mr. Stephanopolous took care of the customers. If I was very fussy, she whispered in my ear, "I love you, little one. I love you just like you were my own grandchild." I, a colicky infant with a brain-damaged mother, was lucky to be the recipient of all that pent-up love.

It was Mrs. Stephanopolous who started my mother's career with a chance comment. Mrs. Stephanopolous had come up to the apartment because she was lonely. Mr. Stephanopolous was visiting a supplier in Burlington, and with no one to cook the lamb lasagna (Mrs. Stephanopolous was terrible in the kitchen, a fact that, she felt, underscored her inability to have a child), she had closed the restaurant.

"How is little Dora today?" she asked, full of expectation, when my mother opened the door.

"With her grandparents, actually," my mother said. "For a few hours."

They stared at each other. My mother was not very good in social situations.

"Well, maybe I would like to come in for a cup of tea?" Mrs. Stephanopolous ventured. It was a habit of hers to phrase requests as though she was speaking another person's lines in a play, prompting remembrance. At Christmas she spoke to Mr. Stephanopolous almost solely in this reflexively interrogative mode. Would I like it if you bought me that coat in the window of Sears? Maybe you should take me to the Ice Capades?

"I have a bottle of wine," my mother said. She didn't drink tea.

Mrs. Stephanopolous was the closest thing my mother had to a friend. Other mothers at the pediatrician's office or the park tried to strike up conversations and my mother chatted pleasantly enough, but there was always a moment of awkwardness, a sense of social uncertainty that undermined the effort. A strangeness. The other women exchanged glances that seemed to say, Well, she's a bit odd, and then the distraction of a child falling off a jungle gym or a baby with a dirty diaper allowed them to move away without promise of coming back. If my mother was hurt by this treatment, she didn't show it. She seemed to understand the very thin line between being alone and being lonely. I don't think I ever saw her cry.

Still, I imagine that Mrs. Stephanopolous, in addition to being a great help to my mother with me, was also someone for whom my mother cared deeply, to the extent that she cared about anyone. It is, after all, quite something to have your landlady pat you on the hand and tell you, if you are worried about your finances, that you are family, and the rent for that month is her Christmas gift to you. Those kindnesses came easily to Mrs. Stephanopolous. Words of praise and encouragement fell from her lips like sugary kisses: I was a beautiful baby, Anna had done such a wonderful job with the curtains, we were welcome in the restaurant any time we liked. So it must have hurt my mother, to the extent that she could be hurt, when Mrs. Stephanopolous expressed horror at my lack of a baby book.

"But Anna," she said, "she is your one precious thing in this world! Is it that you don't have a camera?"

We had a camera.

"Well, is it that you need money to develop the film? I'll give you the money. Do you know how to work the camera? I'll take the pictures myself. Pictures of you and Dora, together."

Pictures held little appeal for my mother.

Mrs. Stephanopolous shook her head. She held my mother's hands. "Anna, these days are going to fly by you and one day little Dora will be grown up. How will you remember her baby days? How will you show her what she was like, so small? All children like that—to see themselves as small babies. To hear the stories of what they were like when they were young." Mrs. Stephanopolous paused, thinking that she might have overstepped the bounds of her own childlessness. She squeezed her crucifix. "You have no idea how lucky you are, Anna. No idea."

I don't think it was coincidence that shortly after this conversation the record of my life on paper begins. My mother started cataloguing my daily activities in a flat, unemotional prose that was tinged with the macabre: Dora ate part of a banana and nearly choked. Dora slipped in the bathtub today and gave herself a black eye. It seemed as though all the important experiences of my early life were linked to death, or its possibility. These moments were privileged over the speaking of my first word (unknown), or my taking of a first step (date unspecified, though event recorded—I nearly fell down the stairs). My mother was not a careless or inattentive parent, and I was not accident prone. It was simply an editorial decision on her part. Death and danger make for clear cause-and-effect relationships. This was a baby book that made sense to her.

The book was especially odd when you took into account my mother's illustrations. She was a frighteningly good artist. She had much trouble interpreting the world but a gift for reflecting it, such was the quirkiness of her condition. Her black ink drawings were heavily shadowed and featured thick, strong, fast lines. The hyperrealism of her style was breathtaking; the camera Mrs. Stephanopolous asked about was completely unnecessary.

It was not, of course, the kind of baby book Mrs. Stephanopolous had in mind, but it proved exceedingly useful for us. When I was almost a year old, my mother brought the book to the restaurant to show Mrs. Stephanopolous, and one of the few regulars in the crowd, a marketing director from Crow Toes Press, happened to be eating the lamb lasagna. His name was Richard Layton.

"Excuse me," he said, wiping his hands on a napkin as Mrs. Stephanopolous flipped the pages of the album. "May I see that?"

My mother, who, to my knowledge, had not considered a career in anything other than temporary jobs at libraries, bookstores, and supermarkets, passed Mr. Layton the album.

He studied it, then me in my mother's arms. Within two years, I was a bestseller.

*   *   *

I NOW UNDERSTAND the pressure to sell, to have a gimmick. Not that long ago I went to a book launch for a novel about boxing. The author fought another man, a poet, from his publishing house. The referee was their shared publicist. The poet beat the living daylights out of the novelist and the crowd got drunk on the free wine and violence, stuffing themselves with greasy finger foods that were served by caterers dressed in athletic gear, headbands and swishy pants. I hear that a lot of books were sold. That was what Richard was trying to do, sell a lot of books, and he succeeded.

He thought it would be a good idea for me to accompany my mother at her promotional readings, the first of which was for a Toronto Public Libraries series called "Kids' World, Real Life." It featured children's authors who, as the brochure stated, presented true-to-life versions of kids' experiences. Richard was all over it.

"We should have been on to this years ago," he said. "Kids are tired of reading about pink elephants and candy cane fairies." Richard was divorced and had no children.

He convinced my mother that I should be there, in my stroller, to help the kids draw the connection between Nora, the somewhat death-marked baby in the books, to "Nora," the real-life child in pink overalls. "Kids are fascinated by the real, Anna. And it's not like Nora would have to do anything. She'd just sleep away in her carriage, and, if you let them, the kids would come up one at a time after the reading to see her. It'd give you something to talk to the parents about. Your mother could take care of Nora, if she cried."

"Dora," my mother said.

"Right."

I don't know why it worked, but it did. Children's eyes goggled back and forth between my mother's illustrations and me sucking my thumb in the stroller or asleep on my grandmother's shoulder, and the realization that I had nearly choked on a banana took on grave significance for them. Perhaps they understood some small degree of their own mortality from this connection: that they, too, might choke on bananas, that life was precarious and dangerous and they were very, very small within it. Perhaps they liked the novelty of a live baby in the same way they enjoyed the novelty of live bunnies and donkeys at a petting zoo. Whatever the reason, the readings, and, more importantly, the books, were a tremendous hit. Richard Layton couldn't believe his luck, and neither could we. After two years, my mother bought everyone presents, starting with her family. There was a king-sized bed for her parents and diamond earrings for her sisters Eva and Marlene. Then music lessons for Eva's son, Marty, as he was having a hard time with his father's death from prostate cancer, and therapy sessions for Marlene, who was bulimic and recently fired from her job as a medical secretary. Breast surgery for Larry as he transitioned into my Aunt Laura, and a new roof for Mr. and Mrs. Stephanopolous' building, the top floor of which we still rented at a ridiculously low rate. Richard Layton was promoted. In so many ways, my mother was able to give everybody exactly what they wanted.

As I grew older, our appearances together became slightly more performative. Richard wanted me to wear the clothes I wore in the books, so my grandmother and Mrs. Stephanopolous worked as competing seamstresses to alter my outgrown clothes. They inserted panels in the backs of dresses, lowered the cuffs on pants, and patched holes in sweaters. If alterations were impossible, they recreated entire outfits. Mr. Stephanopolous helped too, repairing the buckles on a pair of patent leather shoes that are central to *Nora and the Playground Accident.*

I can remember parts of those readings. Hot lights made the pinchy fabric under my armpits even itchier; Mrs. Stephanopolous had trouble fixing the problem of armholes, which my grandmother noted with uncharacteristic smugness. "She sews like she cooks," my grandmother said, helping me wriggle out of a tight sailor suit after a reading at the Toronto Children's Bookstore on Yonge Street. Mrs. Stephanopolous, for her part, criticized my grandmother's liberal use of patches. "What," she said at the Festival of Words, pointing to the off-colour yoke of my dress, "you think our Nora is a little match girl, or something? Make sure you don't let the audience see your back." My mother simply let them dress and undress me. She was confounded by the little doll in front of her who drew a crowd by sitting on a chair, looking like herself.

When I was six years old and Nora was at the height of her popularity, Richard had us booked at the Children's Literature Festival at what was then Young People's Theatre. Mrs. Stephanopolous was with us backstage and she helped me dress in my purple corduroy pinafore, the straps of which my grandmother had spent the evening adjusting. Mrs. Stephanopolous took blush out of her purse and rubbed colour into my cheeks with the pad of her middle finger. "There," she said, giving me her compact mirror. "A little bit happier, don't you think?" I did a little dance for my mother, who clapped softly as I finished. Mrs. Stephanopolous gave me a hug before I went onstage. There was going to be a book signing after. By this time I was an expert at that part of the show, standing beside my mother as small children, many smaller than me, clung to their mothers' legs, once in a while extending a finger to touch the skin on my hand.

I remember that the lights were hot and I was bored, which means it was a typical reading. There was applause, of course, and then the moment when my mother took my hand and we both did a theatrical kind of bow. That was normal. But what stands out in my mind is the part after that, seeing the squirming shadows of the audience as people started to put on coats and zip up purses. For the first time I wondered if they realized how lucky I was, how very loved I was, to have a mother who wrote books about me, who drew pictures of me, each of my freckles, who held my hand under the lights and said, Dora, you've done it again. I bit the insides of my cheeks, sucking at the secret feeling of it all.

"I love you, Mom," I said.

My mother was quite beautiful, even with her scars. She had lips that were naturally bright red. She never wore lipstick, or make-up of any kind, not even under the fluorescent lights, and so when she turned to me, all I saw was that red, that dazzling red, in the whiteness of her face. She walked off the stage, leaving me behind as Mrs. Stephanopolous scooped me up in her fat arms and promised me ice cream, but I imagined myself already full.

*   *   *

I WAS TEN when my mother began dying, fifteen when she finished. Early onset dementia ate into her brain from all sides, likely a result of her accident, the doctors said.

"There are no accidents," I told them.

I was superstitious then and obsessed with Tarot cards. I spent any money I had on readings from Mrs. Lyubitshka, the woman who ran the nearly deserted tea shop half a block from the El Greco restaurant. Only men came into the shop, and then only rarely. If one arrived while I was there, Mrs. Lyubitshka stopped reading the cards and instead made a show of wiping dust out of a teacup and boiling water before she asked me to leave.

"We've broke the flow, Dora," she said in an accent that sounded both Polish and Ukrainian. "You come back, we start again." To the men she said, "Don't worry, she's not my daughter." She said it nicely so as not to hurt my feelings. Then she disappeared into the back room.

The men were usually much older and greyer than Mrs. Lyubitshka, who wasn't more than my mother's age at the time. They reminded me of my grandfather in the way they sometimes held the door as I walked past, tipping their hats at me with great sincerity. I found the gestures quaint and vaguely flattering.

Mrs. Stephanopolous called Mrs. Lyubitshka a crazy gypsy, and Mr. Stephanopolous called her worse. Mrs. Lyubitshka was a bad influence and a poor role model, they said, and they considered themselves entitled to that opinion as my de facto grandparents. They loved me. I had to listen to them. Even my biological grandmother, who was not one to agree with anything Mrs. Stephanopolous said, took her side. Mrs. Lyubitshka was no good.

"A potato gone bad," my grandmother said, wagging her coffee spoon at me. "And you, you are good fruit, Dora." She threatened to cut off my allowance.

My mother had no opinion. She spent her days engaged in increasingly strange pursuits, like colouring in the flowers on the bathroom wallpaper with my marker set, or undressing herself and then watching television. Her skin became nearly translucent and she bruised easily. Once she fainted after cutting herself with a kitchen knife and I had to call 9-1-1. Two paramedics arrived and it took both of them to strap my mother to the gurney. "That's the most blood I've ever seen," the younger one said to me as I sat on the couch in my nightgown. I took it as a kind of compliment. After that Mrs. Stephanopolous packed away the kitchen utensils and disconnected the stove, and Mr. Stephanopolous brought us our meals on trays, checking the pockets of my mother's housedress for rogue forks and knives, which he sometimes found. I remember my mother's hair falling out in alarming bunches when she brushed it. She insisted on doing so until she was nearly bald and my grandmother took away her combs and mine. Mrs. Stephanopolous gave me a very short haircut that made me look like a boy.

"So pretty, Dora," she lied as chunks of my hair coated the kitchen floor. I was not popular at school at this time, and the haircut did not help.

My mother's doctors offered few options outside of hospitalization in a psychiatric ward. We went on a tour of one such facility, my grandparents, Mr. and Mrs. Stephanopolous, my mother, and me. I remember seeing a man in a paper gown masturbating in the hallway. We stayed for lunch. The food was soft and we ate it with plastic spoons. "Careful with these, Dora," my grandfather joked. "They're sharper than they look." In the parking lot, he cried and Mr. Stephanopolous held him, one hand on the back of my grandfather's head. It was the first time I had seen grown men show emotion.

Over time my sets of grandparents, real and adopted, became increasingly occupied with the job of monitoring my mother's behaviour. I was a good girl, they knew. I got excellent grades in math and language arts, and I came home after school and helped with the housework and the errands. Mr. Stephanopolous was teaching me how to cook, and I was a willing student. I also took dictation for my grandfather, who was fond of writing letters to the editors of the major Canadian newspapers and magazines. Other than that, I was left alone much of the time. My mother was a very challenging person for my grandparents to care for. Gradually Mrs. Lyubitshka became the least of their problems.

Mrs. Lyubitshka turned out the cards with the kind of gravity I associated with medical examinations and funerals. It made me feel important that she took my money in exchange for advice on the mysteries of love and fate. She had striking red lips, obviously lipsticked, but against the paleness of her skin, which had a wormlike scar along one cheek, she reminded me just a little of my mother and it was difficult not to stare.

"The cards have interesting things to say to you, I can tell," she said the first time I met her. I was drawn into the shop by the sign out front that said Fortune, Love, Happiness. There was a picture of a glowing crystal ball. I was alone and had an allowance to spend.

Mrs. Lyubitshka sat me down at a wobbly table and closed her eyes. She grazed her fingertips over the cards, now and again bringing one to her chest and holding it against her heart before replacing it in the strange formation on the table. She turned over the first card and told me it was called the Star. The next one was the Lovers. "Your life will have lots of peace, lots of passion," she said. Then there was the Seven of Wands. "Some heartbreak, too."

I was worried, but Mrs. Lyubitshka waved a hand across the table.

"Everyone gets the heartbreak. No big deal."

I also had a lot of blocked creativity, Mrs. Lyubitshka said. Did I paint, or dance? Maybe sing?

I did none of those things. The cards must have made a mistake.

"There are no mistakes," she said, putting the cards into a velvet bag. "Lesson number one of Tarot."

I took these informal lessons from her until I was able to turn out the Petit Jeu without hesitation. At that point she stopped taking my money. Mrs. Lyubitshka helped me develop a kind of patter that she made me practice. It included platitudes for those who were given bad news and cautionary optimism for those with wild good luck. My patter needed a lot of work. I tended towards blunt revelation because I thought it was more honest, but Mrs. Lyubitshka corrected me.

"It's all true stories," she said, "but you need balance for people to believe."

Mrs. Lyubitshka was a kind teacher, and it took years for me to understand the depth of her generosity. A young girl doing her math homework in the window of that shop must have been bad for business, and by the time my mother was hospitalized for good, I was there almost every day.

The money from my days as Nora kept my mother comfortable and, I think, happy until the end. The palliative care facility was a good one, with a courtyard garden and relatively cheerful orderlies who affectionately called my mother Anna Banana as they changed her bed sheets. They were also kind to me. Mrs. Lyubitshka had given me a set of cards to use, and after seeing me deal and re-deal them for my-self, a blonde nurse named Sherry asked me to do a reading for her. She wanted to know if her boyfriend was going to propose. The cards said yes and Sherry said I had a gift. From there I did readings for many of the staff, even though my grandmother said that such paganism was both embarrassing and dangerous. She had long since given up on her first day of spring parties.

I was fourteen before I did a reading for my mother. By that point I had to guide her hand as it cut the deck of cards. I was worried that my touch might influence the result, but my intentions were good, I reasoned, and the cards knew that.

"Try to relax, Mom," I said. My mother was hiccupping quietly and plucking the petals out of a bouquet of daisies Richard Layton had sent her for her birthday. She was perfectly relaxed.

The cards had bad news. My mother turned the Ten of Swords. The picture was of a man with ten swords driven into his back. It signified pain and affliction. She also turned the Tower. The Tower meant any number of things, according to Mrs. Lyubitshka, but it usually meant destruction. Lastly, my mother turned the Death card, which was not difficult to interpret, even for a beginner.

I put the cards away in their velvet bag. I was starting to see that there were limits to what the cards could tell. I was also starting to wonder how Mrs. Lyubitshka made her money.

"I love you, Mom," I said, by way of apology.

"I love you," my mother said to her intravenous bag. "I love you," she said to the pile of flowers on her meal tray. From there we sat silently and she destroyed more daisies.

Sherry came in with a bedpan; my mother told her that she loved her too.

"Isn't that sweet," Sherry said. "Your mom is such a doll." Sherry showed me the diamond ring on her finger and I agreed that it was very pretty.

My grandmother arrived to pick me up, and my mother clapped excitedly.

"I love you," she said. "I love you."

"Yes, Anna," my grandmother said, smoothing her hair, "I know you do."

"I love you, Mom. I'll see you next week," I said, but my mother just stared at me and bit her lips. I waited for a moment more, but nothing came. I waited, for nothing, ashamed that I wanted her to just hurry up and die.

"I'm sorry, Dora," my grandmother said.

"Oh," I said, "it's okay." As if we were talking about an overdue library book or a rental car with poor gas mileage. Something borrowed.

*   *   *

I FELL IN LOVE several times in my twenties, and several men also fell in love with me. It was quite wonderful if the man in question fit into both categories at once, though that happened less often than Mrs. Lyubitshka had led me to believe that it would, and it wasn't happening when I became pregnant.

His name was Henry and he already had a wife. Her name was Isabelle and she was in a coma from a car accident the year before. She and Henry had been driving back from his sister's wedding in Virginia. The sister had married a man who organized Civil War re-enactments.

"You knew it wasn't going to last," Henry told me on our first date. "Kathleen looked so stupid in that hoop skirt."

He and Isabelle had been making a holiday of the trip, stopping at little inns along the way. "We signed the guest registries under fake names and ordered champagne," Henry said, a little embarrassed. "It was a sort of second honeymoon." They had never had a first. Isabelle contracted food poisoning from the chicken kiev at their own wedding reception and they had cancelled the trip to Montreal at the last minute. She lost fifteen pounds in a week, and, according to Henry, she was a tiny woman to begin with.

Henry and I made love in the evenings after he got back from visiting Isabelle. He said there was new research to suggest that a person in a coma still heard and recognized the sound of her loved one's voice, but chattering on about his day made him uncomfortable when all that answered him was the whir of Isabelle's ventilator. Instead he read to her. Borges and Woolf seemed to be her favourites, though he was more partial to Americans, himself. Henry regularly shopped for new books for Isabelle, and I met him in this way, ringing up the sale of *Love in the Time of Cholera*. Afterwards I was embarrassed to admit that I hadn't read it. Henry had read everything, it seemed.

The thing I liked best about Henry was the sound of his heartbeat. He had a rather serious heart murmur, but falling asleep on his chest to the sound of that asymmetrical rhythm was oddly comforting. It gave the illusion of excitement and romance, which we both knew full well was not why we were together. I didn't tell him about the pregnancy, only that I thought we shouldn't see each other anymore. He agreed, delicately, and gave me a copy of *The Heart Is a Lonely Hunter* as a token of his affection, not because it had any special significance for us, but because it was what he had with him at the time and he said he felt the need to give me something.

Having a baby is not as hard as people say it is. The idea of a child is easy to get used to, after a while, and the pain of birth is overplayed to the point of cliché in movies and television programs. It is difficult to be alone, but you can count on your body to do most of the work for you. There are other things you need to worry about. Mr. and Mrs. Stephanop-olous are both dead, as are my grandparents, and it is difficult to think of my daughter growing up without knowing them. I have a close circle of friends, many of whom also have children. My daughter and I go to a lot of picnics and birthday parties. She is still young enough to sleep with me in the same bed, and I put pillows around the edge of the mattress so she won't fall in the night, though she hardly moves, she sleeps so soundly.

My friend Helen and I wheel our children around the neighbourhood in their strollers while they nap in the afternoons. We talk about our work. Helen is writing about highly realistic sex dolls.

"They started out as high-end mannequins, but after a while the manufacturer realized that there was probably money to be made from all the special requests, you know, for orifices," Helen told me recently. "But it's not just about sex."

She said that one man, a widower, ordered two dolls—one to look like his dead wife, and another, a teenager, to approximate the daughter he thought they might have had if his wife hadn't miscarried. The dolls were so lifelike that when he ran errands, the wife doll in the front seat and the daughter doll in the backseat, he had learned to place yellow sticky notes on their foreheads: I am a doll. Before that the wife doll had once slipped out of her seat, slumping over the gearshift, and passersby had called an ambulance to free the woman they thought was dying in the black asphalt swelter of the supermarket parking lot.

I asked if she was serious.

"The paramedics suggested the sticky notes," Helen said. She shrugged. "People are lonely."

We walk until our babies start crying. My daughter's name is Mariana, after both her great-grandmother and grandmother, their names combined. She is old enough now to understand the difference between big and little, bad and good. Her favourite colour is red. She is allergic to penicillin. She is afraid of balloons. She has a doll, a red-nosed clown, and she cries if I take him away from her. I apologize by telling her I love her over and over and over again, by nibbling her ears like a dog. I have learned that there is no such thing as too much love.

Acknowledgements

Thank you to the editors of the following publications, in whose pages several of these stories originally appeared in slightly different form:

"The Party" in *The Fiddlehead* 227 (Fredericton, 2006).

"Strange Pilgrims" in *The New Quarterly* 109 (Waterloo, 2009).

"The Dead Dad Game" in *PRISM International* 47.4 (Vancouver, 2009) and *The Journey Prize Stories* 22 (Toronto: McClelland and Stewart, 2010).

"Poses" in *10: Best Canadian Stories* (Ottawa: Oberon Press, 2010).

"Hurricane Season" in *Grain Magazine* 35.4 (Saskatoon, 2008).

"Monkfish" at www.joylandmagazine.com (Toronto, 2009).

"Problem in the Hamburger Room" in *Canadian Notes & Queries* 82 (Emeryville, 2011).

"Falling in Love" in *Room Magazine* 30.4 (Vancouver, 2008).

"Tick" in *Hart House Review* 17 (Toronto, 2008).

I am indebted to my many teachers and mentors, including Donald Hair, Alison Conway, J.M. Zezulka, J. Douglas Kneale, Tim Blackmore, Rosemary Sullivan, Michael Winter, and the indomitable Larry Garber. Thank you for your patience and your guidance.

This book would not have been possible without the generosity and friendship of my University of Toronto creative writing colleagues, especially Joseph William Frank and Daniel Scott Tysdal. Thank you for sharing your talent and your daring.

Thank you to Dan Wells and John Metcalf for making these stories a collection.

Thank you to Brenda Brooks for her wisdom and her fine-toothed comb.

Thank you to Kathleen Doukas for her friendship across years and oceans.

A special thank you to my dad, Ray, for his unflagging support and loose cannon tendencies, and to my family for their faith and encouragement.

Finally, the most important thank you is for Ian. Thank you for believing in me and in this book, and in our life together.

IAN BROOKS

Laura Boudreau was born and raised in Toronto. She is a graduate of the University of Toronto's MA in English and Creative Writing program. Her short fiction has appeared in a variety of literary journals and anthologies, including *The New Quarterly*, *Grain*, *The Fiddlehead*, *10: Best Canadian Stories*, and *The Journey Prize Stories 22*. Her freelance journalism has been published in Canada, Switzerland, and the United Kingdom.

She currently works in the publishing department of a children's charity, and she lives with her husband in London, England.